"Didn't I see another brother here?" Poppy asked. "He seems to have rushed away."

"You must mean Rye," Thistle replied.

"*Rye*," Poppy repeated, grateful that at least she now had a name for the one with whom she had danced. "Where . . . where do you think he went?" she asked, sensing that she was blushing a little.

Thistle cocked her head to one side and considered Poppy. Then, in a matter-of-fact way, she said, "Rye's always a little weird."

"*Weird?* Why? How?"

"He gets sort of dreamy. You know, he goes off a lot by himself."

"Why . . . why do you think he ran off—this time?" Poppy wanted to know, though she had a fairly good idea.

"He's very emotional," Thistle said. "He loved Ragweed."

Praise for the Poppy books:

AVI

POPPY & RYE

ILLUSTRATED BY *Brian Floca*

HarperTrophy®
An Imprint of HarperCollinsPublishers

Poppy and Rye
Text copyright © 1998 by Avi
Illustrations copyright © 1998 by Brian Floca
The illustrations are drawn with Eberhard Faber Design
Ebony pencils on Stonehenge paper.

Library of Congress Cataloging-in-Publication Data
Avi, 1937–
   Poppy and Rye / Avi. — 1st ed.
     p.   cm.
   Sequel to: Poppy.
   Summary: When their home next to a brook is destroyed by beavers, a large family of
golden mice is aided by Poppy the deer mouse and her grumpy porcupine friend.
   ISBN-10: 0-380-79717-8 — ISBN-13: 978-0-380-79717-2
   [1. Mice—Fiction. 2. Porcupines—Fiction. 3. Animals—Fiction. 4. Fathers and
sons—Fiction.] I. Title.
PZ7.A953Pr 1998
[Fic]—dc21

97-31000
CIP
AC

Typography by Jennifer Bankenstein

❖

Revised Harper Trophy edition, 2007

15 16 OPM 30 29 28

For Us

Contents

THE WOODLANDS

TO DIMWOOD FOREST

NEW HOME OF
THE MICE

OLD HOME OF
THE MICE
x

CANAD

POND

THE DAM

THE LODGE

THE BROOK

OLD PATH OF THE BROOK →

MAIN
LODGE

N E W S

POPPY
& RYE

CHAPTER I

Clover and Valerian

"CLOVER! CLOVER, LOVE. You need to wake up! Something *awful* is happening."

Clover, a golden mouse, was small, round, and fast asleep in a snug corner of her underground nest. Too sleepy to make sense of the words being spoken to her, she opened her silky black eyes, looked up, and gasped.

Was that Ragweed leaning over her? Ragweed was a particular favorite of her sixty-three children. He had gone east in search of adventures but had not been heard of for four months. Clover missed him terribly, and kept wishing he'd come back.

Her eyes focused. She could see more clearly now. "Valerian," she asked, "is that you?"

Valerian was Clover's husband. He was a long-faced, lanky, middle-aged golden mouse with shabby fur of orange hue and scruffy whiskers edged with gray. His face bore the fixed expression of being perpetually overwhelmed without knowing quite what to do about it. At the moment his tail was whipping about in great agitation.

"Is something the matter with the children?" Clover asked. She had recently given birth to a new litter—her fourth that year—and was so tired, she hadn't ventured from the nest in more than a week.

"They're fine," Valerian assured her. "But Clover, you've got to see what I've discovered. You've not going to believe it."

"Can't you just tell me what it is?" Clover replied with a yawn. She never got enough sleep.

"Clover," Valerian whispered, "we're . . . we're in great danger."

A startled Clover looked about the nest where she and Valerian and all their children had made their home for six happy years. A small, deep, and comfortable nest consisting of three chambers, each of its rooms was lined with milkweed fluff. There were a family room, a master bedroom, and the children's nursery, where thirteen of the children were currently sleeping. The most recent litter— three in number and barely a week old—were still blind and without fur. They were with Clover.

"Clover, love," Valerian urged, "please get up. It's *not* the children. But it will affect them. Badly."

With Clover, an appeal to family never failed. She forced herself up.

The two mice made their way up the entry hole to the ground surface. The long, twisting tunnel had a few storage rooms—one filled with nuts, another with dried berries, a third with seeds—built into the walls. Though Clover was, as usual, hungry, there was no time to eat.

When Valerian reached the ground's surface, he stuck his nose out of the entry hole, sniffed, then gazed about. Certain there were no foxes, wild cats or snakes, or any other danger about, he hauled himself out of the hole. Clover followed.

Tall, leafy trees, bushes, and brambles veiled the late summer sky, a sky aglow with the light of a full moon. The air was humid, the breeze soft. Barks and buzzes, grunts and chirps seemed to come from everywhere and nowhere all at once.

Valerian scampered down one of the many paths that radiated from the nest. When he took the path that followed a

steep decline, Clover knew they were heading for the Brook.

"The Brook," as the mice called it, meandered lazily between low, leafy banks. Water lilies floated on its wide, shallow surface. There, fireflies flashed, butterflies danced. Mosquitoes, like ancient instruments, droned. Water bugs scooted. Cattails, standing tall, swayed to the rhythms of the night.

With nothing rough or dangerous about the Brook, the young mice loved to frolic about its banks. Rarely was the water more than six inches deep. Splendid to splash in. Fun to swim in. Sometimes the mice made rafts of bark chips and went boating. Indeed, it was the closeness of the Brook and its serenity that caused Clover and Valerian to build their nest and raise their family where they did.

That night everything was changed.

The water was muddier and deeper than it ever before had been. A full three feet of bare earth at the base of the pathway—the children's beach—had sunk beneath water. Lily pads and cattails were gone. No bugs teased the Brook's surface. Chips of wood floated here, there, everywhere.

"Look!" Valerian cried, in a hushed voice. He pointed downstream.

At first Clover didn't see it. Only gradually did she perceive the massive mound of sticks, twigs, and logs that spread across the full width of the stream.

"Why . . . my goodness," she gasped. "It's a . . . *dam*! But . . . but why?"

Valerian pointed to the water's edge.

"What should I be looking at?" asked a puzzled Clover.

"The water," Valerian whispered. "Watch."

Clover stared until, with a shock, she jumped back. "Valerian," she cried, "the water is rising!"

"Exactly."

"But . . . if it keeps coming this fast, our home will be . . . flooded!"

Valerian nodded. "Clover, love, I'm afraid the whole neighborhood is going under."

"But . . . but," Clover stammered, "who would do such a dreadful thing?"

"Take a gander out there," Valerian urged. This time he pointed across the water.

Clover stared. At first she thought she was seeing nothing more than a floating brown lump of earth or wood. Then, with a start, she realized it was an animal swimming on the water's surface.

He was a large, portly fellow, with thick, glossy brown fur, a black nose, and two beady eyes. Two enormous buck teeth—brilliant orange in the light of the moon—stuck out from his mouth like chisels.

"A . . . *beaver*!" Clover exclaimed. Just to say the word brought understanding: Beavers had come and dammed the Brook.

As Clover and Valerian stared, the beaver saw them. Lifting his water-soaked head, he offered an immense, toothy smile.

"Bless my teeth and smooth my tail!" the beaver called out in a loud, raucous voice. "I do believe it's my new neighbors! Hey, pal! Evening, sweetheart! Tickled pink to meet up with you. The name is Caster P. Canad. But everybody calls me Cas. Hey," he added with another toothy grin, "you know what the old philosopher says, 'A stranger is just a friend you haven't met.'

"As for me, I'm head of the construction co that's doing the work here. Canad and Co. 'Progress Without Pain,' that's our motto."

"But . . . but . . . you've . . . destroyed our brook," Clover managed to say.

"Easy does it, sweetheart, easy does it," Mr. Canad boomed with insistent good nature. "Don't need to make a mountain out of a molehill, do we? Or for that matter," he added with a laugh that set his belly to shaking, "an ocean out of a puddle."

Without saying another word, Valerian and Clover turned and fled back up the path.

6

"Have a nice day!" the beaver shouted after them, though it was the middle of the night. "I mean that, sincerely!"

As the two mice dashed toward their nest, all Clover could think was, "Oh, Ragweed. Please, please come home. We need you! Where are you?"

CHAPTER 2

Poppy and Ereth

It was cool in Dimwood Forest. Through the high canopy of trees, flecks of sunlight sprinkled the earth with spots of gold. But on the floor of the forest, inside a long, hollow, and decaying log, it was all stink and muck.

"Oh, skunk whizzle," mocked the old porcupine who lived in the log. "Who cares foot fungus about Ragweed's family? I bet they're nothing but nasty nose bumps."

Though his full name was Erethizon Dorsatum, the porcupine insisted on being called Ereth. Not the sweetest smelling of creatures, he had a flat face with a blunt, black nose and fierce, grizzled whiskers. Sharp quills covered him from head to tail.

He was talking to a deer mouse by the name of Poppy.

Though most of her fur was soft orange-brown, Poppy had pure white fur on her round, gracefully plump belly. Her whiskers, which stuck straight out from her delicate pink nose, were quite full. Her toes were small and her tail was long. As for her ears, they were relatively large and dark, and from the right one hung an earring, nothing more than a purple plastic bead dangling from a tiny chain.

"Ereth," Poppy explained, "if something happened to a child of yours, wouldn't *you* want to hear about it?"

"Look here, slug-brain," the porcupine said with something close to anger, "I thought you liked living in my neighborhood. Thought you were *my* friend. But if you want to trundle off, forget me, make new friends, start a new life, go ahead. I've got plenty of things to do."

"Like what?" Poppy asked.

"Eating," the porcupine growled. "And sleeping." With a rattle of quills Ereth moved off toward the far end of his log.

"Ereth," Poppy pleaded as she followed after him, "let me try to explain one more time. Ragweed was a golden mouse. He was like no one I'd ever met before. And when he came here, I fell in love with him."

"*Love!*" sneered Ereth. "You can put love in a wasp's nest and chew on it."

"But I *did* love him," Poppy insisted. "And we . . . we were going to get married."

"*Marriage!*" Ereth hooted. "Head for the toilet bowl and bring two plungers!"

"But then," Poppy continued patiently, "that owl, Mr. Ocax, killed him and—"

"Poppy, stop! I've heard this slop a hundred times!"

"But all I want to do," an exasperated Poppy continued, "is tell Ragweed's parents what happened to him. Don't you think they should know? Besides, I want to give them this." She touched the earring. "So they'll have something to remember him by."

"Listen, swamp-mouth," Ereth said, "take my word. They don't care what happened to him. No more than I do. Wise up. You'd have to be mushroom mucus not to know that!"

"The thing is, Ereth," Poppy persisted, "the trip would be so much nicer if you came along. It'll be an adventure. We'll see the world."

"Oh, frozen frog pips!" Ereth cried. "I don't *want* to see the world. I hate going places. I hate doing things. And I *like* being alone. Most of all, I'm sick and tired of hearing about Ragweed! So beat it!" The porcupine continued on toward the far end of his log.

A frustrated Poppy let out a sigh, tenderly fingered Ragweed's earring, then went to the open end of the log and gazed out at Dimwood Forest.

This forest of towering trees was her home. One moment it was dark, the next moment it was light. Usually serene, the forest often exploded with noisy life. Though Poppy loved the forest dearly, and would miss it, she felt a great need to make the journey.

Poppy had to acknowledge that there was no particular *reason* for Ereth to go. He had never met Ragweed. Besides, Poppy hardly knew where his home was. Ragweed had never offered much detail about it. "The Woodlands," he called his home area. He said it was a few miles west of Dimwood Forest.

His family nest, he had once told her, was on the banks of a brook. He referred to it as little more than "The Brook." "It's a decent spot, girl," Ragweed had told her. "But, know what I'm saying, like, dullsville. Totally. Nothing ever happens there."

"Tell me about your parents," Poppy had said to him.

"They're named Clover and Valerian," he said. "Pretty cool . . . for parents. But, hey, like, I needed to see the world. And I did, too."

"Did they give you permission to go?" Poppy asked, impressed with Ragweed's story. At the time not only hadn't she gone far from where her own family lived, she was certain her parents would never allow her to travel.

Ragweed laughed. "Naw, they weren't too easy 'bout what I was doing. Particularly Clover, my old mouse. But girl, a mouse has to do what a mouse has to do."

"Will you ever go back?" Poppy wanted to know.

"Oh, sure, someday. And hey, dude, I'll take you there," Ragweed promised. "Bet you'll like my folks. They'll think you're way sweet."

"Why?"

"'Cause you're my main girl, girl!" Then—Poppy remembered—Ragweed had winked at her with a sense of his own saucy being.

But Ragweed had died. And Poppy wanted to tell his parents what had happened. Maybe, she mused, it was her way of saying a final good-bye to the mouse she had loved.

Still, to go all that distance alone would be quite an undertaking.

It was not that Poppy was frightened of the distance or of being alone. It was merely a question of wanting to go *with* someone. True, she had plenty of sisters and brothers—cousins, too, for that matter. Still, she could think of no better companion for an adventure than her best friend, Ereth. But now the porcupine had said no. Poppy sighed. There were moments she actually thought Ereth was jealous of Ragweed.

Then the notion struck Poppy that it was probably nothing more than Ereth feeling his age. How like Ereth to be so proud he wouldn't admit to such a thing. She wished she had not pushed him so.

Never mind. Poppy made up her mind: Since she wanted to go, she'd go alone.

Oh, well, she thought, I'm sure I'll meet *someone* interesting. Besides, once I get to Ragweed's brook it should be pleasant and calm. Recalling his words about the Brook, Poppy smiled. I could use a little dullness in my life, she thought.

Poppy went back into the log to say good-bye to Ereth. He was at the far, smelly end, licking a hunk of salt as if it were a lollipop.

Trying to keep from inhaling too much, Poppy said, "Ereth, I wanted to say good-bye."

The porcupine offered up an indifferent grunt.

"And Ereth . . . I should apologize."

"What for?"

"Asking you to come."

Ereth paused in his licking and squinted angrily down at Poppy. "Why?"

"I should have remembered you're too old for such a trip."

The salt dropped from Ereth's paws with a clatter. "Too *what*?" he gasped.

"Well, you know," Poppy said with care. "Elderly."

"Me? Old? Elderly?" the porcupine cried, quills bristling. "You twisted bee burp! I can do whatever I want. Where I want. When I want. Or are you hankering to turn yourself into a busted bee bottom?"

"But, Ereth . . ."

"Look here, you pickle-tailed fur booger," he roared on, "I can keep up with you any day of the week. Night too, for that matter, you slippery spot of squirrel splat!"

"You mean you'll come with me?" Poppy cried, trying to keep from grinning.

"Blow your nose and fill a bucket!" Ereth screeched. "Can't you understand *anything*? Never mind me going with *you*. You're going with *me*!"

With that, Ereth burst past Poppy, moving so fast, so furiously, his quills combed her belly fur into twenty-seven neat rows.

Poppy, laughing, ran after him.

CHAPTER 3

Night Thoughts

ERETH MOVED ALONG so fast Poppy had to race after him. Her cries of, "Hey, slow down! Wait for me!" were of no avail. Only when they reached the deepest part of Dimwood Forest did Ereth finally pause.

When Poppy caught up to him, the porcupine was calmly nibbling on some tender bits of bark which he had peeled from a tree.

It was a dusky place. The high trees kept the light out but not the heat. The air felt as thick as syrup and bore a smell of skunkweed and rotting mushrooms.

"What is this spot?" a panting Poppy asked, throwing herself down on the ground to rest. Though she had always known Dimwood Forest was big, she was beginning to fathom just how small a part of it she'd experienced.

"The forest," Ereth replied smugly.

"Amazing," Poppy said, staring around.

"Now, look here," Ereth said, "where was it that

you said we were going?"

Poppy, still breathing hard from her exertion, said, "It's called The Brook."

"Oh, fox flip," the porcupine growled. "There must be a million brooks in this forest! Are you saying that's the only name you have?"

"Ereth," Poppy said, "all Ragweed told me was it was west of the forest.

"Sticky roach toes," Ereth muttered. "According to that, it could be anywhere."

"No, it can't," Poppy pointed out. "It's not east. Or north. Or even south. It's *west*." She looked toward the sky. Though the sun was hidden behind heavy foliage, it was still possible to find its place in the sky. "Since it's afternoon," she said, "west must be that way."

"Fine," Ereth conceded. "But how are we supposed to know *which* brook it is?"

"Ereth," Poppy said, "we don't need to have all the answers, do we? Can't we just keep moving? We've got all the time we need."

"The faster we get there, the faster we get back," Ereth returned.

Poppy got up and started off, this time taking the lead. Ereth, muttering "Ragweed" under his breath, followed.

The two friends traveled side by side. Moving in a steady,

westerly direction, speaking little, they did not stop until darkness came. They had not come upon one brook.

"I think we'd better find a place for the night," Poppy suggested. She was quite worn out.

"When I travel, I stay in trees," Ereth informed her.

"That's fine with me," Poppy assured him. "Pick out one you'd like."

"Can't be any tree, you know. Has to be comfortable."

"Fine."

"Right height."

"Good."

"And smell right."

"Just choose one, Ereth!" Poppy cried.

Constantly grumbling, Ereth lumbered about the forest floor, examining every tree he passed. Poppy followed, pausing now and again to nibble seeds when she found them. It made little difference to her where she slept. As long as she was with Ereth, she was safe. Nobody wanted to mess with him or his quills.

The porcupine finally settled on a fat tamarack pine. Its branches were thick. Its smell was pungent.

Moving awkwardly from branch to branch, Ereth climbed. Poppy followed.

Halfway up the tree, Ereth came upon a particularly fat branch whose broad width at the point where it grew out

of the main trunk made a platform. "I suppose this'll do," he said, and settled down.

"Mind if I snuggle in?" Poppy asked.

"*Snuggle*," Ereth mocked. "Why don't you just say, 'mind if I lean on you?'"

"I prefer *snuggle*," Poppy said with a grin. She settled herself between Ereth's front paws, curled up in a ball, and took a deep, relaxing breath.

Though the air was ripe with the sticky scent of pine, Poppy detected the smell of nearby blossoms. Loving flowers of any kind, she was happy.

The night was full of noises, too. She heard the soft,

padded steps of animals, the slithering of snakes, the piping of frogs, the chirping of crickets. Now and again leaves rustled in the breeze. The night is dancing, she thought.

The stars seemed so distant. How far, Poppy wondered, would she have to travel to reach one of them?

Letting slip a murmur of contentment, she nestled closer to Ereth. She was perfectly aware he was not the easiest of companions, but she loved him for the good, blunt friend he was. Besides, whether he meant it or not, he kept her mind off the sad part of this journey, the meeting with Ragweed's parents.

So far the trip was exactly what she had wanted. She could already sense her grief easing. She was convinced that once she saw Ragweed's parents and delivered her doleful news—and his earring—she would be able to return home and get on with her life. The thought soothed her. She began to drift off to sleep.

Ereth broke the silence. "Poppy," he growled, "when you tell Ragweed's parents what happened to him, I won't be around."

"Oh, why?" Poppy said with a yawn.

"Because it's just family fripple, that's why. I hate all that garbage."

"Ereth, you can do what you want."

"I do," Ereth said. "Always."

"Fine."

Poppy yawned again, and closed her eyes.

Then Ereth said, "It's all those stupid *feelings*. Porcupines get along without that bunk."

"Not *one* feeling?"

"For salt . . . maybe."

When Poppy made no response Ereth added, "It's better that way."

"How come?" Poppy asked sleepily.

"Oh, chipmunk cheese. It . . . just is."

Poppy was too tired to debate. Instead, she pondered what she might say to Ragweed's parents, wondering if they would blame her for his death. Yawning, she placed her tail under her nose, and was soon fast asleep.

Ereth stared into the dark. "This is dumb," he said to himself. "I never should have come. *Ragweed*," he sneered. "Nothing but Ragweed. Nothing but sugared mouse slops. Phooey!"

CHAPTER 4

The Water Rises

THE BEAVERS BUILT the dam higher. Inch by inch the water rose. It licked the low banks then swallowed them whole. It crept and crawled and poked into every crevice, filling them up. It trickled along animal paths and washed them away. It sank flowers and grasses and turned them into soup. It slid between bushes and trees and drowned them, root, leaf, and branch. It made islands of low hills. It flooded nests. The water was unstoppable.

Though Clover and Valerian could observe the water rising with their own eyes, they found it hard to accept that their nest was doomed. After all, they had lived in one place for years. During that time how many storms had they weathered? How many droughts? How many cold winters? To all questions, the same answer: many.

"Why are the beavers doing this?" the children asked.

"Be fair," Valerian said with a catch in his throat and a harassed look on his face. "We don't own the Brook, do we? Don't you think beavers have as much right to live here as we do?"

"But their pond is getting huge!" one of the children objected. "It's taking over everything!"

Valerian sighed. "Maybe I can talk to them."

So it was that Valerian—feeling apprehensive, trying to keep his gray whiskers neat—crept down to the shore of the newly created pond.

The old brook had been surrounded by many trees. The new pond was encircled by chewed-off and jagged stumps. The old brook had been tranquil. The new pond fairly rattled with beavers hard at work. Even as Valerian stood there he heard the sound of yet another tree crashing. He winced.

"Hello!" he called out across the pond. "Can I speak to someone?"

One of the beavers paused to look around. "Hey, old timer, what's up?"

"I'm fine, thank you," Valerian returned politely.

"Who are you?" the beaver asked.

"I . . . I live here."

"Do you? That's cool. What's happening, pal?"

"I'd like to speak to Mr. Canad."

"Cas? He's probably busy, but I'll go check."

The beaver dove, leaving Valerian to pace nervously, tail waving in agitation.

Within moments Mr. Canad burst up to the water's surface. "Hey, pal! Nice to see you again," he cried out. "Don't think I got your name."

"Valerian."

"Val. Right! What's up, pal?"

"Well, sir, it's this . . . pond you're building."

"Sight for sore eyes, isn't it?" the beaver boomed.

"Well, I was just wondering . . . how . . . I mean, no one *owns* the Brook. So, of course, naturally, we're obliged to share. But we . . . well, we were wondering just how . . . well . . . big you intended to make it."

"*Big?*" Mr. Canad cried. "Tell you something, pal, you ain't seen nothing yet! Talking world-class pond here. The

cat's pajamas and meow in combo. Over the top! Major league. The whole enchilada. Hey, Pal, Canad and Co. don't *do* small."

"But," Valerian said plaintively, "if you make it too big . . . you'll drive us folks who live here . . . away."

"Look here, Pal," Mr. Canad said, "I'm telling you, I'd be tickled pink to see you stay. You seem decent. Clean. Good manners. Not a troublemaker, are you?"

"No, sir."

"Great! Glad to have you around! 'Progress Without Pain.' That's our slogan. But, if you have to move, well, hey, no problem. Have a great trip. *Ban voyage. Hasta la sweeta. Are revor.*"

"Can't we compromise?" Valerian pleaded. "So we can both stay?"

"Pal, I've put quality time into that question. Comes to this: Beavers do what beavers do. There you are: Question in, answer out. Neat as a pin. Hey, nice talking to you, pal. Appreciate it. Really do. Have a nice day! I mean that, sincerely!" he cried, and dove beneath the water.

Valerian, more discouraged than when he went, returned to the nest.

"What did they say?" his children asked.

"We have to move."

So Valerian and Clover began a frantic search for another suitable home. It was not easy. In the best of times good nests were hard to find. Now they had waited too long. Many creatures—caught in the same predicament as they—were already gone. When the mice finally found an acceptable new home it was on a hill, cresting the ridge overlooking the new pond: a small, damp hole with a large, cold boulder for a roof.

The boulder was perched precariously atop the hill. As Valerian considered it, he worried that it wouldn't take much to set it rolling. That brought nightmarish visions of its tumbling away in the night, leaving his children exposed.

Clover sighed. "It'll have to do."

"I reckon it will," Valerian agreed, trying to hide his worries.

Neither one mentioned that fitting thirteen children into one dank, chilly nest was going to be difficult.

Yet even after they had found their new quarters, they put off moving. It was too painful. Only when water began to trickle down their long entryway and make puddles in the middle of their main room did they finally pack their belongings.

These belongings—already mildewed and sodden— were easy enough to gather and haul out of the tunnel. Much harder was the removal of their children.

"Do we *have* to move?" the first complained.

"But Ma!" said another. "What about my friends?"

"The water isn't *that* bad," said a third. "We can make rafts. Build a houseboat. Swim from room to room. Be cool."

And a fourth: "Do you really, really, really, *really* promise we'll come back when the water goes down?"

"Dear, dear children," Clover said, trying unsuccessfully to keep back her tears, "we have to go."

Of those children who still lived at home, Rye was the eldest. Like all the golden mice, he had fur of an earthy orange color, a tail that was not very long, small, round ears, and youthful, downy whiskers. He did have a small notch in his right ear, but that was the result of a childhood accident.

Rye had never left home. He claimed he stayed behind to help his parents with the youngsters. Others suggested it was because he enjoyed being the eldest—which he

became once Ragweed had left.

"Rye," Valerian said, "take yourself and some of your siblings and go search out the rest of the family. Let them know your mother and I have moved to higher ground. Tell them where."

Rye's chest swelled with pride that it was he who had been called upon to inform his far-flung family about what was happening.

Thistle, his by-one-litter younger sister, squeaked, "Do we have to go to *everybody*?" She wasn't even sure how many brothers and sisters she had.

"Absolutely," Valerian insisted. "All sixty-three."

"Now do hurry, Rye," Clover said. "It's urgent!"

Hearing the distress in their parents' voices, Rye, Thistle, and a younger brother, Curleydock, sped off to do as they were told.

Later that day, the family moved. When the children were all out of the nest, Clover and Valerian took one last, lingering look about their old home. Side by side, she short and plump, he tall and thin, they held paws.

Suddenly, Clover said, "Valerian, what about Ragweed?"

"What about him?"

"Who's going to tell him where we've gone?"

Valerian pulled his whiskers. "Clover, love, I'd say that when and if Ragweed gets back he'll see for himself that things are changed. That's all."

"What do you mean *if?*" Clover asked tremulously.

"Just saying, if ever we had a smart child, it's Ragweed. He'll find us when he comes looking."

Clover and Valerian scampered out of the nest.

Within hours their old home was entirely under water.

CHAPTER 5

Some Words
Are Exchanged

THE DAY AFTER they moved, Rye, Thistle, and Curleydock crouched beneath a tangle of blackberry bushes and
looked out over the pond.

"There's one!" Rye hissed.

A fat beaver had climbed atop a particularly large mound

of sticks in the pond not far from the dam. It was dumping and smoothing mud on the mound's surface.

"That's their main lodge," Rye said with authority, though it was Valerian who had informed him of that fact only the day before.

"How do they get into it?" Curleydock asked. As the family went Curleydock was on the small side, and rather plump like his mother.

"There's an underwater passageway," Rye said. "You have to swim deep to get in there."

"Cool," murmured Thistle. Tall and sleek, with swept back whiskers and narrow ears, she was a good swimmer.

"It's not cool," Rye said sharply. "They have no right to come and just take over everything. Look what happened to our nest." He waved a paw over the water. "Gone. You call that cool?"

Thistle shrank down. "I was just saying the beavers' home is . . . *interesting.*"

"Look!" Curleydock whispered.

Three beavers had surfaced near the shore. They tumbled and turned, smacking the water with their large, flat tails.

"Big, aren't they?" Thistle said, her voice full of awe.

"They look like they're having fun," Curleydock said wistfully.

"Fun!" Rye snarled under his breath. "I hate them! I'd

like to give them a piece of fun!"

"When Ragweed gets back, he'll do it," Curleydock said. "He's not afraid of anyone."

"Ragweed's gone," Rye snapped. "Besides," he went on, "who needs him? *I'm* not afraid of them."

Thistle stared at her elder brother with wide eyes. "You mean you'd . . . talk to them?"

"No big thing," Rye replied.

"Except Ragweed wouldn't *say* he would," Curleydock said, and snickered. "He'd just *do* it."

Rye felt hot. "So would I."

"Dare you," his brother goaded. "*Double* dare."

Rye, suddenly nervous, said, "I'll do it if you come with me."

"You first," Thistle replied.

Rye considered the beavers anew.

"See," Curleydock said. "I told you. You're no Ragweed."

Rye offered his brother a dirty look, then crawled out from under the berry bush. Wanting his heart not to beat so fast, he yanked his whiskers—he wished they were darker, stiffer—licked down the hair on his chest, then headed down toward the water, tail tucked between trembling legs.

Halfway to the pond, Rye halted. "You coming or not?" he called back, hoping he sounded cocky.

Thistle scampered to her brother's side. The two checked back.

"Well?" Rye asked.

Curleydock crept forward.

The three mice inched to the water's edge near where the three beavers were playing. The beavers paid them no attention.

"Go on, tell them what you think," Curleydock said, giving Rye a nudge. "You know, the way Ragweed would."

Feeling he could not back down, a jittery Rye cupped his front paws around his mouth to make himself heard. "Hey you!" he shouted.

The beavers halted their play and looked about with dripping muzzles. "Were you speaking to us?" one of them asked.

"You're the ones who dammed our brook, aren't you?"

The beavers exchanged looks. One of them paddled through the water until she was close to the mice.

Her orange front teeth were enormous. The three mice retreated a few steps.

"My name is Clara. Clara Canad. What's yours?"

"Rye."

"Something bothering you, Rye?"

Rye took a breath. "You beavers just barged into our neighborhood and . . . and . . . took over. Ruined the Brook!

Ruined the land! Ruined our nest! You're thoughtless and greedy."

"Hey, fellah," Clara retorted, "making a pond is progress."

"Progress?" Rye cried. "Progress for you, maybe. What about the rest of us? Who invited you here, anyway?"

"No one invited us," Clara replied. "Do you mice own this brook?"

"Well . . . no."

"There a sign posted, Reserved for Mice Only?"

"No, but . . ."

"And it's still a free country, isn't it?"

"I suppose . . ."

"Well, then, don't you think we've got the right to build our lodges here?"

"But it's *not* right!" a confused Rye cried. "You destroyed *our* nest!"

"Hey, sorry to hear it," Clara returned. "There's always a price to pay for progress."

"But who's paying that price?" Rye screamed. "*We are*! The ones who live here. You just flood, flood, flood!"

"I'd be more than happy to talk to you in a civil way," the beaver returned, "but if all you can do is rant and rave, I'd just as soon not listen." She turned about, and as she drew away she lifted her tail and brought it down hard and flat upon the water, sending out a great spray that thoroughly soaked the mice.

Sopping wet, the mice ran off. But not before Thistle stopped and shouted back at the beavers. "You just wait till my brother Ragweed comes home," she cried. "He'll fix you!"

CHAPTER 6

Rye

THE POND-SIDE meeting with the beavers had infuriated and humiliated Rye. It wasn't only the beavers that had upset him. It was all that talk about his brother Ragweed.

Rye loved his elder brother. A lot. Admired him. Looked up to him. But if Ragweed wasn't teasing Rye, he was lecturing him, telling him the best way to do something, saying Rye was doing something wrong. Rye chafed under such treatment. Despised it.

So there were times Rye was quite sure he hated Ragweed, too. It seemed that no matter what he did, his whole family—mother, father, brothers, and sisters—was holding Ragweed up as the best. Rye was sure they were always comparing *him* to Ragweed. Unfavorably. As far as Rye was concerned, it wasn't fair. "I'm not Ragweed," he continually reminded them. "I'm *me*."

It didn't help that Rye and Ragweed looked so much alike. Though a few months younger than Ragweed, Rye was just as long and thin, and had the same sharp, penetrating gaze and noble nose. The way most knew how to tell the brothers apart was that small notch in Rye's right ear.

But whereas Ragweed was blunt, even cocky, Rye was considered the more thoughtful mouse, something of a dreamer. "A romantic," Clover said, with a wistful shake of her head.

Rye often wandered nearby meadows, where he liked to fling himself under a flower and daydream of romantic adventures.

When he returned—flower in paw—and was asked what he'd done, he'd reply, "Oh, nothing. Some thinking, I suppose."

"But what were you thinking about?"

"Today? Oh, the sky, clouds, and . . . flowers."

It was only when Ragweed left home that Rye came into his own. Now *he* was the eldest of the children at home. Now the younger ones looked up to *him*. Now his parents called upon *him* to do things. *His* opinion was asked. *He* was heard.

Yet, even as that happened, Rye feared things would remain that way only until Ragweed returned. Hadn't Curleydock said as much when Rye tried to speak to the beavers?

Hardly a wonder then that, as far as Rye was concerned, there were moments he hoped Ragweed would *not* come home. Of course he wouldn't *say* anything like that. The thought made him feel ashamed. It seemed unnatural, sinful.

So it was that after he shouted insults at the beavers and was splashed away for his efforts, Rye returned to the family's new nest in a deep sulk. To make things worse, no one seemed to understand why he was sulking.

"What's the matter with Rye?" one of his younger brothers asked Thistle.

"Just daydreaming."

"He's always daydreaming!"

Later that day Valerian called upon Rye to join him while he went to forage for food. A reluctant Rye heaved himself up and went along.

Father and son went out behind the boulder and took a path that led them to an old patch of sunflowers. The flowers had been planted years ago by humans—or so the mice believed—and sunflowers had grown upon that spot ever since. The great, round, yellow blossoms, like so many tethered suns, nodded and bobbed. Even better—as far as the mice were concerned—it was a fine place for sunflower-seed gathering.

Rye and Valerian had gathered a fair pile of seeds when Valerian asked, "What's the problem, Rye? You're acting kind of droopy."

"Oh . . . never mind," Rye mumbled.

"You sure?"

"Well . . . yes." Rye, who always assumed no one would listen to him, found it hard to express himself. In that, he wished he *were* more like Ragweed. Ragweed always told everybody exactly what he was thinking.

Valerian sat down, leaned against a stump, put a blade of grass in his teeth, and adjusted his arms behind his head. "This business of the beavers, the Brook, and all they've done—it's upsetting. It is. Still, the family has done pretty well, considering. 'Course, your mother has been grand. Always is. You do know what a fine mother you have, don't you, son? Lovely creature," he murmured. "Truly lovely."

"I suppose. . . ." Rye said. He sat down next to his father.

"Truth is," Valerian continued with a rueful shake of his head, "it doesn't seem like there's much we can do. Beavers are big and powerful. They don't want to listen to us. I'm just hoping they stop building. Now of course—" Valerian's voice trailed off.

"Of course . . . what?" Rye asked.

Valerian threw the grass blade away and reached over to their seed pile. He looked it over, selected a seed, polished it against his chest, then took a bite.

"What?" Rye prompted.

"Oh," Valerian finally said, "your mother doesn't say, though it does slip out now and again. I'm fairly sure she thinks that when Ragweed comes home he'll solve every-

thing." He contemplated the seed in his paws.

Rye stiffened. "Do *you* think so?" he asked, ready to bolt up and walk off.

"Nope," his father said. He took another bite of the seed and chewed thoughtfully.

"You don't?" said Rye, taken by surprise. "Why?"

Instead of answering, Valerian remained quiet and stared off into the distance. Now and again he nibbled at his seed.

"Well, son, it's a big world out there. Full of possibilities. Dangers. Your brother isn't shy. He likes getting into things. Seems to me, if he was coming back, well, he'd have done so by now." There was a tremor in his voice.

Shocked, Rye looked around. "Do . . . do you think something . . . happened to him?" he asked. Something in his world shifted.

At first Valerian only nodded. It took a moment for him to speak. "Don't know for sure, of course, do I?" There was another pause. "But well, I've got this . . . bad feeling."

"But . . . that would be awful," Rye said, gazing at his father's sad face. Yet hadn't he almost wished for it?

"Yawp, it'd be pretty sad, all right," his father said.

"Do you . . . do you think," Rye said, "I should go and look for him?"

"Nope," Valerian said. "Ragweed could be anywhere. If he's coming back, he'll come in his own sweet time.

Besides, we don't want you disappearing, too."

Rye hesitated before saying, "Why?"

"We need you, Rye," Valerian said. "We need you a lot."

Rye almost burst into tears of gratitude. But then he asked, "Does that mean that if . . . if Ragweed did come back, you . . . *wouldn't* need me?"

"Son," Valerian said, "all I'm saying is, I don't think Ragweed is coming back."

Rye, however, noticed that his father had not really answered his question: What would *Rye's* place be if Ragweed returned? Disappointed, he did not want to ask again. His thoughts were already too confused.

That night Rye could not sleep. Wedged in amidst his family in the one-room nest, he kept thinking about his talk with his father. What had happened to Ragweed? Would his brother come back? What would happen if he did? In particular, Rye wondered what would happen to *him* if Ragweed came home? Would he be ignored again?

The more Rye thought about it, the more unappreciated he felt. He forgot how wonderful it had been when his father had talked to him mouse to mouse. Instead he thought, "Pa was telling me not to go off only because Ragweed is gone."

It was but a matter of moments before Rye was saying to himself, "Who pays attention to *me*?" He answered his own question quickly: "Nobody!"

Perhaps, he thought, it *would* be a good thing if he went off to look for Ragweed. When he found him, he'd tell his brother he was needed at home. Then Rye could go off and have his *own* adventures.

On the other paw, Rye mused, if he could not find Ragweed, but could discover what had happened to him, he could bring *that* news to his family. Not only could they be at rest with the matter, he could take his permanent place as the eldest child at home.

It was the middle of the night. The whole nest was asleep, except Rye. He got up quietly. There were no particular belongings he needed or wanted to take. Still, he thought it best to leave something to tell his parents where he was going. They might even think he was doing something brave as well as useful.

Finding a pale leaf, he wrote a good-bye note:

Dear Mom & Pa,
Farewell!
I've gone into the great world to search for Ragweed.
Fear not! I shall return!

Your devoted son,
Rye

Rye took a deep breath. The night was balmy, sweet with the smell of growing things. The moon appeared calm in a velvet black sky. The grass was soft beneath his toes. The whole world seemed full and ripe.

Rye's slim chest swelled with emotion. Oh, to have something important happen to *him* at last! Oh, to be noticed, to be told by someone, "Rye, how glad I am to see *you*!"

Yet was he, Rye kept wondering, doing the right thing by going? I'm doing it for the family, he told himself. It has nothing to do with me at all.

With that thought firmly embedded in his heart, Rye set off. He was heading due east.

CHAPTER 7

Mr. Caster P. Canad and Company

The beavers' lodge was a large, domed structure made of sticks and twigs, plastered over with mud. To get inside the lodge the beavers—just as Valerian had informed Rye—had to swim through an underwater tunnel.

Though a small vent hole at the top of the dome provided some fresh air, it was hot and humid inside the lodge. The little light there was came from the sporadic flashing light of fireflies, which the beavers had snared and brought into the lodge for just that purpose.

Standing at the far end of the lodge was Mr. Caster P. Canad. Looking around, paws contentedly folded over his pot belly, he liked what he saw: twelve beavers, family all, sitting on their tails paying close attention to him. Wife, child, cousin, brother or sister, he treated them all with total equality. That is to say, he was everybody's boss. He offered up a ripe, toothy smile.

In one of Mr. Canad's paws was a branch—a pointer. Next to him was a large sheet of bark, which he had attached to a wall. The bark bore a drawing of the new pond the beavers had created.

"All right then," Mr. Canad began, tapping his stick against the drawing. "Here's where we've constructed the dam. Mighty fine dam, too, if I do say so myself. Yes, sir, when Canad and Co. builds a dam, we don't let the grass grow under our feet, do we?"

"Way to go, Cas," murmured a few of the beavers, slapping their tails down on the mud floor of the lodge by way of approval.

"Okay," Mr. Canad continued, "every journey begins with a step. But it's plain as the nose on your face, we're going to build the biggest, best, most profitable pond in the whole country. Honest to goodness, as the day is long, take my word for it, we are. You know what the old philosopher said: 'If you can't see the forest for the trees, chew the trees down!'

"Okay. Good news and bad news. The good news is that so far we've done a fine job on the pond. Peachy keen-o job." Mr. Canad tapped the map with his stick. "Bad news," he went on with a good-natured chuckle, "Rome wasn't built in a day, either.

"Which reminds me. . . . Has anyone come up with a

good name for this project? The locals call the brook, The Brook. Hey, dull as ditch water. Can't sell lodges by calling them The Brook. Far as I'm concerned, it doesn't hit the nail on the head."

"Hey, Cas," one of the beavers called out, "what about Wet Wonderland?"

"Or, Welcome Water World," suggested another.

"Mud Flats," offered a third.

To each suggestion Mr. Canad offered up a toothy smile. "Fine. Fine," he said. "Keep those thinking caps on. Those names are A-OK. What we need, though, is something

that hits folks square in the eye. Something strong. Dynamic. That goes over the top. Scores a bull's-eye. Is a hole in one. The whole ten yards. A knock out in one. Slam dunk. I'm telling you, straight from the heart, there's nothing I admire more than originality. As long as it fits the bill.

"So, sure as the sun rises in the morning, I put on my thinking cap and came up with—this should knock your front teeth cockeyed—Canad's Cute Condos. Says it all, don't you know. Canad's Cute Condos. Has a solid ring to it, wouldn't you say? The real plastic."

There was a general thumping of tails.

"Okay. We agree. From here on out, we call this project Canad's Cute Condos.

"Now," Mr. Canad continued, using his stick to clarify his ideas, "with the dam built *here*, Canad's Cute Condos will extend its boundaries. Here. Here. Here. How do you like them wood chips?" He grinned, exposing his orange buck teeth to the fullest.

Tails thumped.

"As for lodges, we'll scatter them here, here, here. Plus a few more canals over here." Mr. Canad pointed to different places on the bark.

"I know this is a lot of work. But don't forget the turtle, the hare, or the Alamo. We don't want to let the grass grow under our feet. Which is okay, except we want *water* under our feet. The more the better. If there's one thing I can tell you, Canad's Cute Condos will be *wet*.

"My loyal, hard-working company," Mr. Canad continued, "we're the original eager beavers. Canad and Co. has never shied from hard work. Never will. Yes, sir, if better ponds are to be built, Canad and Co. will build them! Any questions?"

One of the beavers raised a paw.

"Yes, Clara."

"I have received a complaint about what we're doing here. Rather rudely put, too, I'm afraid."

Mr. Canad nodded sagely. "Hard to believe, sweetheart, but there are those who want life to go on the way it always has. Can't stand progress. Resist it.

"Okay. Let's be sensitive to these folks. Pity them. They don't understand they're sitting right smack dab in the middle of the future. So, be patient, but get on with the job. Be understanding, but don't give an inch. Keep saying 'Progress Without Pain,' till they believe it. Anyway, little folks can't do much about us. Not by a long shot. Or a short one," he added with a chuckle.

"What if they make trouble?" asked one of the other beavers.

"Okay. I've been around the pond a few times. Talk is cheap. Actions speak louder than words. A flat whack of the old tail solves most problems. Hey! The bottom line is, we've got bigger bottoms."

The lodge rippled with laughter and a few tail slaps.

"All right then," Mr. Canad concluded. "Don't have to remind you, there's work to be done. I'll be by your side. Don't want to hear about any beaver who isn't busy. Hang in there. Be fresh as a daisy. When the going gets tough, the tough get going. And finally, from the bottom of my heart, and from the top, as well as the sides and also the middle, I want to say to you all, and I mean this, really, I do, with all my soul, honestly, *sincerely*, have a nice day!"

CHAPTER 8

A Dance upon the Meadow

POPPY AND ERETH continued traveling west. Though there were many trails from which to choose, there were no clear signs to follow. The best that Poppy could do was to keep them moving in a westerly direction. For Ereth, it was a point of pride to refuse to ask directions from anyone.

"But why?" Poppy wanted to know.

"Ask for directions and you're admitting you're helpless," the porcupine pronounced. "The only thing that matters is that I know my way back home."

When they did meet other mice, voles, a badger—once a deer and her fawn—it was Poppy who asked for advice. "We're looking for the Brook," she would say. "Do you have any idea where that might be?"

The other animals were more than obliging. When these fellow travelers knew where a brook was, they explained

how to reach it. And Poppy and Ereth did find them: one or two large brooks, some three of smaller size. But no golden mice were to be found.

"Ereth," Poppy finally said, "we don't seem to be getting any closer to where Ragweed said his family lived. Do you think he might have been confused about which way he came?"

"Probably," Ereth grumbled.

"I admit," Poppy confessed, "I'm beginning to wonder how much longer we should go on."

Ereth came to a quick stop. "Fine," he said. "Let's go home."

The anxiety in his voice caused Poppy to consider him thoughtfully. "You've been awfully quiet lately," she said. "Is something bothering you?"

"Oh, sparrow swit," Ereth barked. "Can't a fellow keep his thoughts to himself?"

"Of course he can."

"Look here, Poppy," the porcupine said, "I'm not used to being with others. How many times do I have to say it, I *like* being alone."

"That's fine," the mouse returned. "I was just wondering."

"Well, stop wondering, puzz ball."

"But the forest does seem to be thinning," Poppy pointed out. "Maybe we are closer to those woodlands."

Ereth looked about. "I prefer the dark," he said.

Poppy sighed. "I'm going on a bit more."

"Do what you want," Ereth growled.

By midday, with the trees thinning more and more and the sun beating down hard, it became too hot to travel. Ereth announced he needed a nap. Without even waiting for Poppy to reply, he rattled off the trail, found a shady spot in a tree, curled up in a ball, and went to sleep.

Poppy rolled over on her stomach, plucked a blade of

grass, and chewed it meditatively.

Before her spread a small meadow. Surrounded on three sides by trees, it had a closed-in, secure feeling. The grasses were low, sprinkled about with flowers. She noticed yellow viola, forget-me-nots, and bluebells. There was a scarlet falsemallow and some lovely, lush poppies.

A black and orange butterfly came into view, fluttering its wings like a slow-motion dancer. Soon after a fat bumblebee, legs bulky with golden pollen, worked its way from flower to flower. A fast dancer, Poppy thought.

As Poppy looked on, something stirred within her. To her surprise, she felt lonely and empty yet full and content all at once. How, she wondered, could she feel such contradictions?

Then, as she watched a dragonfly dart by, she recalled that it had been a long time since she had danced. When she was young—a few months ago—she had thought a great deal about dancing. She even had wanted to be a dancer.

Sighing, she recollected that she never had danced with Ragweed. They had meant to. Now she felt the desire to dance again.

With a nervous glance up at Ereth to make sure he was still sleeping, she got to her feet.

Poppy checked a second time to make sure her friend was asleep. She was in no mood to deal with the porcupine's teasing. When he didn't stir, she lifted her front paws as if to pluck the sun from the sky. Her tail began to wave to a steady beat. A miniature melody, halfway between a whistle and hum, rose to her throat. It was no particular tune, just *something* she made up then and there.

She took one step, and another, gliding forward, pretending, wanting to be as graceful as possible. With every step her heart seemed to lighten.

Within moments Poppy was leaping about, skimming the surface of the field, bending and bowing, twirling and whirling, hardly thinking, aware mostly of the sun's warmth that caressed her fur, and the cool grasses that tickled her toes. Oh, how she loved to dance! Oh, how she loved life!

Almost overwhelmed with emotion, Poppy closed her eyes, spun, dipped, and danced some more. Then she opened her eyes. Standing before her was a mouse.

Poppy gasped. For one indescribable moment she

thought it was Ragweed. The mouse before her had the same orange-colored fur. His whiskers were fair. His tail was not very long. His ears were small and round. She almost cried, "Ragweed!" but could not find tongue to do it.

Then she noticed a small notch on this mouse's right ear. This was *not* Ragweed. Even so she stood there, transfixed, staring, heart pounding as fast as hummingbird wings.

For his part, the strange mouse stood absolutely still, gazing at Poppy as if in a rhapsody.

When Poppy had opened her eyes she had been in the midst of a twirl, arms and paws extended before her, legs behind. As she gawked at the mouse before her she dared not move.

Now the strange mouse extended *his* paws. Without a word, he gently took Poppy's paws in his. At his touch Poppy felt a tingle ripple through her body. It was as if a feather had stroked her from her tail to her nose.

For a moment—a moment that felt like eternity—the two mice looked into each other's eyes.

He whispered, "May I dance with you?"

In answer, Poppy made the first move. It was not a movement away, or a retreat, but a small step to one side.

His paws in hers, the two mice moved in perfect rhythm. Round and round and paw-in-paw they danced upon the meadow. Eyes locked, whiskers sometimes brushing, they turned this way, that way, bobbing, bowing, soaring, in as graceful a duet as two mice ever had danced, could dance, would dance.

How much Poppy wanted to ask, "Who are you? What are you? Where do you come from?" She could not. She had no voice or words capable of expressing what she felt. She only knew nothing bad was happening. Indeed, it was just the opposite. Something very fine was occurring, something grand, something *wonderful*!

Suddenly, Poppy slipped. Her paws jerked away from the stranger's paws and she fell back. The two mice continued to stare at one another.

The other mouse blushed, turned, and fled toward the West, disappearing amid the trees that surrounded the field.

A speechless Poppy stared after him, even as her questions returned: Who are you? What are you? Where do you come from? *Where are you going*? But the other mouse was gone. Poppy had no answers.

Overwhelmed, Poppy picked herself up from the ground. Half walking, half staggering, she made her way back to where Ereth had remained, asleep.

At the base of the tree she sat down and closed her eyes.

Had it all been a dream? Or had something truly extraordinary occurred?

She was not sure.

The next thing Poppy felt was her shoulder being rudely shaken. Simultaneously, she heard Ereth splutter into her ear, "Let's go, stink foot. The sooner we get to where we're going, the sooner we can get back home."

But what had happened to Rye? For it was Rye with whom Poppy had danced.

He had gone from the meadow in a stupor equal to Poppy's. As he went he paused now and again to look back longingly. "Who are you? What are you?" he asked the image of Poppy. "What is your name? Where do you hail from? Where will you go?" And why did he feel he had to go away, when in fact he wanted to go back and dance forever?

Rye also asked himself if the dance had been real or only a moment's fantasy.

So intent was he upon these questions that he completely forgot he was running away from home. When he did remember, he had already reached the entryway to the family nest under the boulder. "Oh, well," Rye said dreamily, "I might as well stay."

No one had noticed he had gone.

CHAPTER 9

The Rain Falls

Poppy and Ereth trudged along in silence. With her mind taken up by thoughts of the mouse with whom she had danced, she was grateful for the quiet. How so very much like Ragweed he was! And yet—how different. While they looked alike, the stranger seemed softer, gentler than the bold, headstrong Ragweed she had known. Certainly this mouse was more romantic. Was he, Poppy kept wondering, a dream or not? If he was a dream, he was the best dream she'd ever had. Still, she hoped he was real.

If her dance partner had been real, how could she find him again? Of course it was impossible that he had been Ragweed. But the mouse clearly was a *golden* mouse. If there was one golden mouse in the area, perhaps there would be others. Did that mean she was nearing Ragweed's home?

As they walked, Poppy hummed the snippet of tune she had composed for her dance.

So preoccupied was Poppy by her musings that she failed to notice that Ereth was frowning and grumbling even more than usual.

"What's that noise?" he suddenly asked.

"It's me, humming."

"I'm in no mood for music."

"How come?"

"I . . . Oh, forget it."

Poppy paused to look at her friend closely. There was a look in his eyes she had never seen before. "Ereth," she said, suddenly alarmed. "What is it?"

Ereth looked a little sheepish. "I . . . well . . . bumblebee flunk. Never mind!"

Poppy offered a worried glance but chose to ask no more questions. In any case she preferred to think about her dance. Once again she began to hum her tune.

The two friends continued west. When on occasion they met others on the path—a mole, a water rat—Poppy asked if they had ever heard of the Brook. Much advice was offered, directions were given, and sure enough another brook was found. Small and calm, it was very much what Poppy imagined she was looking for. To her disappointment no golden mice lived thereabout.

A resident otter did inform Poppy and Ereth that there was another pretty, shallow brook, no farther than two hills beyond, in "that" direction. The otter pointed due west.

"I bet we find the right one this time," Poppy, ever hopeful, said to Ereth as they started again.

Ereth grew even more gloomy.

Though the day had begun bright and clear, the sky had turned gray and cloudy, the air heavy. Treetops flicked and bobbed in a humid breeze. Birds flew high and fast. Clearly, a storm was coming.

With new urgency, Poppy and Ereth trudged toward the crest of the second hill.

"Maybe when we get to the top we'll see the brook that the otter mentioned," Poppy said.

"Soon as we get to the top of that hill," Ereth proclaimed, "I'm going back home."

"Why?"

"I'm sick of walking," the porcupine replied.

From the crest of the hill they looked down into a valley. At the very bottom was a pond.

"No brook," Ereth said with palpable relief. "Let's go home."

"Well, actually," Poppy pointed out, "there's a brook leading into the pond. And out of it."

Ereth muttered something unintelligible under his breath. Then he said, "It's going to rain."

"Ereth," Poppy said, "rain won't hurt us. I'm going to

check that brook."

Even as they stood, drops began to fall. At first it came slowly, great plops of water. Then, while lightning crackled off to the distant north and thunder followed, a steady drizzle began to fall.

Ereth wheeled about and moved toward a clump of trees.

"Where you going?" Poppy called.

"Where do you think, toad-wart? Out of the rain."

"Ereth, I want to explore that brook!"

"Buzzard fraps," the porcupine muttered.

Poppy watched Ereth go. "Will you promise to stay there until I search a bit?" she called after him.

"I never promise anything."

"How will I know where you are?"

"Watch my tracks."

Poppy waited until Ereth reached a cottonwood tree and started to climb it. She noted its position, then hurried down the path. By now the rain was falling steadily.

For his part Ereth looked around, saw which way Poppy was going—down the other side of the hill—then curled himself into a tight ball and closed his eyes. "I never should have come," he muttered. "Ragweed. Nothing but Ragweed. I thought I was her best friend."

Poppy was approaching the pond. Halfway down the hill she could see that it had been created by beavers. At one end was a dam, and Poppy could even observe a number of beavers hard at work. Some were swimming upon the pond's surface. Others were laboring on lodges. A few were working on the main dam, building it higher.

At the far side of the pond a particularly large, fat beaver was gnawing upon the trunk of an aspen tree. There was a sharp crack as the tree snapped and tumbled to earth, landing with a crash.

At the sound all the beavers in the pond looked around. When they saw it was a tree that had fallen, they began to slap the pond's surface with their tails.

Poppy, standing in the rain, looking on, heard someone say, "Awful. Just awful."

She turned. Sitting beneath a large toadstool, protected from the rain, was a golden mouse.

Poppy's heart fluttered. For an instant she thought it was the one with whom she had danced. Then she saw that this mouse, though tall and thin, was a female.

"Hello," Poppy said.

The mouse looked beyond Poppy. "Oh, hi," she said. She sounded unhappy.

"Do you live around here?" Poppy asked.

"Yes."

"Are there . . . are there a lot of you around?" Poppy inquired. "I mean . . . *golden* mice."

The mouse looked down at herself as if she had never considered the question before. "I suppose."

"My name is Poppy," Poppy said. "I'm a deer mouse."

"My name is Thistle," said the other. "How come you're standing in the rain?"

"Oh, right. I am. May I join you?"

"Sure."

Poppy darted under the cover of the toadstool. Thistle, making room, asked, "Where are you from?"

"Back east. Over by Dimwood Forest."

"Never heard of it," Thistle said with polite indifference. She had turned back to stare down at the pond. Water dripped from around the edges of the toadstool like a tattered curtain.

"I hate beavers," Thistle said.

"Why?"

"When they made that pond they ruined everything for everybody. The Brook used to be so cool."

Poppy's heart gave a lurch. "Is that what you called it?" she asked, her voice faltering. "The Brook?"

Thistle nodded. "You wouldn't think it used to be small and calm. Look at it now!" she said sadly. Then she added, "Our home was right on the banks of the Brook. No more. Flooded out. We had to move away. Because of them."

Poppy was trying to restrain her growing excitement.

"Thistle . . ." Poppy said nervously.

"What?"

"Does the name . . . *Ragweed* . . . mean anything to you?"

Thistle had been gazing mournfully down at the pond. At the name she whirled about. "*Ragweed!*" she cried. "That's my brother! Do you know him? Have you seen him? Have you any idea where he is? Is he coming back? I can't tell you how much we need him!"

Instead of answering Thistle's barrage of questions, Poppy asked one of her own. "Are your parents named Clover and Valerian?"

"How did you know? Ragweed must have told you. But that means you *do* know him. Oh, man, you gotta see my parents. Our nest isn't far," she went on. "Come on. Please tell me about Ragweed. What's he doing? You don't know how much we miss him! Do you know when he's coming? We really need him to come back. I've got tons of brothers but Ragweed's the *best*."

Managing to push down her emotions, but speaking in a strained voice, Poppy said, "I think I better talk to your parents."

Thistle darted into the rain. "I'll take you. What did you say your name was?"

"Poppy."

"Poppy, you won't believe how glad my parents will be to see you!"

With Thistle looking over her shoulder to make sure Poppy was following, the two mice made their way through the rain along a path that led uphill from the pond. The farther they went, the more nervous Poppy became.

"It's just over here," Thistle kept calling.

They had come to a large boulder embedded in an out-cropping of earth. A variety of shrubs and flowers rimmed the rock. In the rain they seemed shrunken and cold.

Poppy herself was thoroughly soaked as well as trembling. The wetness came from the rain but the trembling

came from her emotions. Though Thistle was just as wet, she was too excited to notice Poppy's state.

"Just follow me," the young mouse said, darting along the base of the rock, then plunging into the small hole which was screened by some flowering rosecrown.

At the entry hole, Poppy paused to give herself strength. "Why did I ever want to do this?" she wondered.

Thistle popped back up out of the hole. "Come on!" she called, then plunged down the tunnel again. A reluctant Poppy followed at a slower pace. She could hear Thistle yell, "Ma! Pa! Everyone. Guess what? Someone's come with news about Ragweed!"

Full of dread, wishing the tunnel were a hundred miles long, Poppy crept the whole way. All the same, within moments she entered the nest.

In a glance Poppy saw the nest for what it was: a single, shabby room stuffed with golden mice. Golden mice tended to be bigger than deer mice, so Poppy's first sensation was not only that there were a lot of them, but that they all seemed quite large.

But Poppy had not the slightest doubt she was in the presence of Ragweed's family. The resemblance was uncanny. It was as if she were in a room full of familiar ghosts. She felt weak.

There were the two adults, Clover and Valerian, plus

eleven children. The children ranged from fully grown young adults to squeaking infants, one of which was being burped on Clover's shoulder.

When Poppy entered the nest the golden mice stared at her with twitching ears and wide eyes.

"This is Poppy," Thistle announced excitedly.

"How do," Valerian said, standing tall and thin, and fussing with his whiskers. There was a tremor in his voice.

Clover, very pale, said nothing. Her black eyes, open wide, just stared at Poppy. Her whiskers were shaking.

Thistle cried, "Poppy knows all about Ragweed, don't you?"

Poppy was so choked with emotion, it was all she could do to nod a response and gaze from face to face. Suddenly, she stopped. At the back of the pack was the mouse she had danced with. There was the same sweet, soft, noble face, the same right ear with a notch.

Their eyes met—and held. Poppy's heart fluttered. Grief, joy, relief, sadness—all mingled, but in such confusion she hardly knew *what* she felt.

She lowered her eyes.

Valerian, his voice husky, spoke out. "My dear Miss mouse, *do* you have some news about our son, Ragweed?"

"Yes . . ." Poppy managed to say.

"What's . . . happened to him?" Clover blurted out.

"When . . . when is he coming home?"

Poppy found it impossible to speak. Instead she sought out the face of her dancing partner. Once again their eyes met. How she wished he were not there. How she wished she were not going to say what she had to say.

"Please," she heard Clover beg as if from some distant place. "I really must know." As Clover spoke she stood up—infant still in her arms—and reached a paw to touch Valerian, as if she were in need of steadying. Her round, heavy body seemed uncertain on her stumpy legs.

Poppy turned back to Clover. "I'm afraid Ragweed . . ." The next word stuck. She could not speak the word. She had to force it out. "Ragweed is . . . dead," she finally said, her voice tiny.

Utter silence.

"*Dead?*" a small voice, a youngster's, echoed.

"Dead?" Clover repeated.

Poppy could only nod yes.

Valerian cleared his throat. "But . . . *how?*" he managed to ask.

"An owl killed him."

"An owl . . ." someone said. Then all was silence again.

Suddenly Clover sat down. "My own poor, sweet boy," she sobbed.

"Can you tell us more?" Valerian asked in a choked voice.

Poppy closed her eyes. When she opened them she sought out the face of the mouse with whom she had danced. When she found it, it was full of awful sadness. "We . . . we were . . . in love," Poppy said. "We were going to marry."

"Oh, my," Clover murmured, putting a paw to her trembling lips.

Valerian swallowed hard, cleared his throat, and said, "Poppy . . . I . . . we thank you for coming and . . . telling us." He wiped a tear from one cheek, then the other.

"I thought you'd want to know," Poppy said softly. "That's why I came."

The golden mice stared at Poppy as if she had spoken a strange language. Clover, letting escape a small squeak, even as she stroked the baby she was holding, said, "It's a terrible thing to live beyond your own children."

With great effort Valerian drew himself up. "Poppy, it was generous of you to come so far to bring us . . . the news. You must be tired."

"I'm all right," Poppy said.

"You're welcome to stay with us as long as you like," he added. "This is not . . . where Ragweed was brought up. We've fallen on hard times. But . . . our nest is your nest."

"The beavers sank our nest," one of the young mice shouted. All the children began to talk at once.

"Poppy, I must ask you something . . ." Clover suddenly said. In an instant the nest became quiet again.

"Yes, please," Poppy said.

"I hope you loved my son very much," Clover said.

Poppy did not answer right away. Instead, she looked down at her toes, then up and around, seeking the face of the one with whom she had danced. He was gazing at her with a look of profound pain.

"*Did* you love him?" Clover pressed. The question seemed urgent.

"Yes," Poppy said, "I did. Very much."

"Oh, my dear . . ." Clover cried. Thrusting the baby she'd been holding into Valerian's paws, she rushed over to Poppy and gave her an engulfing hug. Poppy hugged her back. As she did, she saw, from the corner of an eye, the mouse she had danced with, his face awash with grief, rush past and fling himself up the tunnel.

CHAPTER 10

Ereth Has Some Thoughts

Hunched on his perch in the cottonwood tree, Ereth stared gloomily at the falling rain. Lightning crackled overhead. Thunder rumbled. The world had become gray and sodden.

"I hate water," Ereth proclaimed to nobody in particular. "In fact," he muttered, "I hate everything."

Again and again he wished he were back home in his smelly log in Dimwood Forest. It was dry there. It was quiet. He was alone. Nothing—no one—bothered him.

"Whatever made me come here?" he kept asking himself. "Poppy did. She forced me to come. . . . Mouse frickets . . ." he muttered. "Double mouse frickets. *Quadruple* mouse frickets!"

From directly over his head, a pool of water that had collected in the fold of a leaf fell on his face.

"That's enough!" Ereth shouted with a furious shake of

his head. "I'm going home!" Snarling and hissing, he scrambled down the tree. Once on soggy ground, he paused. The storm appeared to be growing worse. The rain was falling harder and faster. If he went he would get soaked. Then a wind shook the tree, causing a cascade of water to plop on his head. He moaned. If he stayed he would get soaked. Where was that foolish mouse? Why did he ever bother with her?

"If I go it will teach her a lesson. If I teach her a lesson she'll get upset with me," he told himself. "If she gets upset she'll scold me. Then I'll feel bad. Why should I care? She's just a friend. No," he corrected himself. "I have no friends. I don't want any friends. Poppy's just an acquaintance. A passerby.

"Poppy!" he bellowed. "Where are you? Why don't you come back? I need . . ." He bit off the rest of his sentence. "Spider spit," he swore out loud. "Sticky, slimy, sloppy, spider spit!"

Furious, he jumped out from under the tree, only to sink knee-deep in mud. Complaining bitterly, he shook his paws free. "Maybe Poppy's coming now," he thought. "I'll meet her halfway. Make her hurry. Tell her to stop all this drivel about Ragweed. Ragweed. . . ." He growled. "I *hate* Ragweed."

He tore down the path he had seen Poppy take. As he went the rain came down harder. Water poured over his face. He felt like a decaying mushroom. "Stupid storm!" he shouted.

He peered down the path. There appeared to be nothing before him but water, mist, mud, and more mud. The porcupine shivered violently, making his quills rattle like a bag of old bones.

"Better go back to that tree and wait for her there," he decided. "It was a little drier there."

He started off the way he had come, only to stop abruptly.

"This isn't right," he growled with rage. Spinning around, he lumbered in another direction, trying to catch the scent of his own tracks. It had vanished. The rain had washed it away.

Lost, increasingly frustrated, Ereth galloped first this way, then that in search of the cottonwood tree. "Duck dapple!" he shouted up at the clouds. "Dry up!" But the rain continued to fall.

Utterly wretched, Ereth peered through the gloom until he saw a stand of trees that he thought would protect him. He ran forward.

Reaching the trees was easy enough. But *which* tree should he climb? Confounded by his own anger, he rushed from one to another. The first was too small. The second was too thin.

Seven trees later he found one to his liking. The bark was rough. The foliage was thick. Frantic, Ereth clawed past the first layer of branches, the second, and the third. "This'll do," he muttered, moving toward a particularly large branch.

He reached it and squatted down, trying to make as tight a ball of himself as possible. Even so, the rain pelted him.

"Stupid mouse . . ." he mumbled. "No, she's not stupid. She's mean. What kind of friend would leave me in all this muck? She's abandoned me. Left me. When I'm her real friend. Her only friend. But no, all she thinks about is Ragweed. Who's *dead!* As for me, she keeps telling me I'm old. *Old!*" he shouted. "I'm not old! Don't I take care of her, help her, love . . ."

He stopped. "Love . . ." he muttered. "I don't love Poppy. I hate Poppy!" he shouted. "I hate love!"

Bursting with rage, the porcupine scrambled down from his tree and began to gallop as fast as he could. Where he was running he had no idea, no more than he knew if the water dripping from his cheeks was rain or . . . something else.

CHAPTER II

Mr. Canad Makes Some Plans

It was still raining. In the middle of the pond, Mr. Canad used his webbed feet to propel himself swiftly across the water with strong, steady strokes. There was something mighty fine about swimming, enough to make one fit as a fiddle.

Now and again he lifted his head and let the pattering rain soak him even more. "Bless my teeth and smooth my tail," he murmured. "I do love water!" Then he thought hard as to how best to express his feelings in words that had a real impact. Though it took some hard thinking, he worked it out. "The whole thing is," he decided, "it never rains but it should do it a lot."

When Mr. Canad said the phrase out loud, biting off the last T with his large orange teeth, he enjoyed it so much he repeated it to himself: "It never rains but it should do it a lot—a lot.

"I must use that," he told himself. "Perhaps during the next company meeting. They would appreciate it. They would."

With his strong paws Mr. Canad pulled himself onto the bank, gave himself a shake—sending water in all directions—then turned to survey what had been achieved by the beavers' work.

In the little valley through which the Brook had flowed there had been, in Mr. Canad's mind, a dull, dreary landscape, with little to behold but a piddling stream without power or grandeur. It had no depth. Its banks were wasteful in their simple, sloping nature. Why, the water itself had no texture or color. One could see through it!

Limpid lily pads and useless bulrushes had marred its lazy surface. The animals who had wasted their time on the banks—mice, voles, otters, and toads—were insignificant. As far as Mr. Canad was concerned, it had been a place where nothing important ever had or would happen. An utter waste.

But now, how different the beavers had made it! Every day the pond was growing wider, deeper, grander. It had taken on the vibrant color of mud. It was a home for hearty, busy beavers who worked day and night.

"This," Mr. Canad said to himself with genuine pride, "is

progress." The portly beaver felt so good about it, he spelled the word out letter by letter: "P-R-O-G-R-E-S-S!"

And yet, Mr. Canad had to confess, he was not fully satisfied. No, he was not. What he and his company had created was—he had to admit it—merely a pond.

Mind, he told himself, there was nothing wrong with a *pond*. A beaver who built a good pond had every reason to be pleased with himself. Yet even the word *pond* suggested smallness, a compactness of size which might be good enough for some, but not for the likes of Caster P. Canad and Co.! Not only could they do better, they *should* do better. As Mr. Canad saw things, it was not a pond that was needed but a *lake*!

The beaver cast his keen engineer's eye over the little valley. To achieve a lake they needed to build another dam higher up.

As he surveyed the little valley, he noticed a boulder perched on a hill. A large boulder, it was embedded in an outcropping of earth and stone. Flowers and shrubs shaded it. As Mr. Canad perceived it, the boulder was doing *nothing* but sitting there. But it could be providing the perfect anchor for a new dam. An immense dam! With a dam at that spot, a large lake could be created. It would be his crowning achievement, a monument to himself. Indeed, what could be a better name than Lake Canad? Mr. Canad liked the sound of it so much he said it a few times.

Then he reminded himself, with some gleeful rubbing of back feet, that it was time to stop dreaming. Time to get down to the nitty gritty. To grasp the nettle. To get into the trenches. To show the flag. To hit the road running.

But even as he watched and planned he saw a mouse creep out from under the boulder and rush away.

Mr. Canad knew what that meant: Mice were living under the boulder. As far as he knew, these mice were the only ones left around the brook. Most of the other creatures had departed. How pleasing to know there had been no resistance. Surely these last mice would quickly see the hopelessness of resisting the future. But what if they did not?

He could swat them away. Mere nothings that they were, squashing the mice would be easy, though the thought made Mr. Canad uncomfortable. He was no bully. He just wanted progress. He wanted the world to appreciate him for the good he was doing. What he needed to do was find a way to convince the mice to leave—of their own accord. It would make him feel good. Nothing was more important than to make good their slogan, "Progress Without Pain."

Mr. Canad dove back into the pond and made his way to the main lodge. When he came within five feet of it, he dove and swam underwater until he found the entrance.

Mr. Canad went to his plans—laid out on bark—and began to draw in detail. The boulder here. The large new dam there. The lake . . . everywhere.

Then he mused, "If I can make a lake, well, bless my teeth and smooth my tail, why not an *ocean?*"

The thought made Mr. Canad grin broadly. Then he said, "It never rains but it should do it a lot. On me."

Then he gave himself over to finding a way to convince those last few mice that they should move away.

CHAPTER 12

In the Nest

IN CLOVER AND
Valerian's nest under the
boulder there was nothing
but despair. Poppy's news of
Ragweed's death had devas-
tated the family. The coming
of the beavers, the damming of
the Brook, the creation of the pond,
their change of homes, all of that had been difficult to
accept. But the family had shared the notion—spoken and
unspoken—that Ragweed would return and somehow,
some way, sort things out. Poppy's tragic news made it perfectly clear that no such thing would happen.

Everything was now worse.

In one corner of the nest sat a disconsolate Clover, staring off into nothing that anyone else could see. From time
to time she let forth a profoundly deep sigh and shifted her

bulk—as if gathering her last breath in her chest. Though her black eyes were dry, they held such a weight of wretched pain, it alarmed her own children.

When a child brushed by—it always seemed like an accident but it happened often—Clover reached out and touched it gently. Sometimes she stroked it. But there was little life or spirit to her paw.

As for Valerian, though he was just as heartbroken as Clover, he spent his time and energy trying to comfort the children. "Your mother will be fine," he kept telling them. "She's just very sad. And it *is* sad."

The children did notice that now and again Valerian wiped his cheeks with the back of his paw, or blew his nose so loudly it sounded like the honking of a goose heading south. "Summer colds are stupid," he kept saying. No one pointed out that he had had no cold before Poppy's news.

Those children who remembered Ragweed best sniffled, wept in corners, or exchanged reminiscences, trying, with little success, to keep their grief private or to keep a brave face.

Then they got it into their heads that it was their parents who needed to be consoled most. Not knowing what to say, they did what they thought was the next best thing: They did whatever they were asked to do and some things that they were not asked as well—did them so fast they almost tripped over themselves in their desire to please. So they were constantly cleaning up, sweeping the entry hall, minding the infants, preparing meals—anything they could think of that might soothe their parents. Someone was always sweeping, straightening up, or burping babies. . . . The result was a continual low hubbub that got on everybody's nerves.

If two of the youngest mice got into a scuffle—they didn't quite grasp what had happened—it was their elder brothers and sisters who stepped in and stifled the discord.

"Please," they whispered. "Clover is very sad." Or, "Valerian is crying." This so alarmed the youngsters that they sniffled and whimpered and clung to their parents more than ever.

As for Poppy, she hardly knew what to do or say. No one asked her to do anything. No one asked her to leave. On the contrary, they had assured her that she should stay. She was stared at a lot, as one who had a particular connection to Ragweed and his awful death and thus seemed extraordinary. Still, no one inquired about *her* feelings, *her* life. She felt as useless as an extra tail.

She did find time to take Thistle aside, and ask, "Was I wrong, but didn't I see another brother here? He had a notch in his right ear. He was standing way in the back, behind you all. He seems to have rushed away."

"You must mean Rye," Thistle replied.

"*Rye*," Poppy repeated, grateful that at least she now had a name for the one with whom she had danced. "Where . . . where do you think he went?" she asked, sensing that she was blushing a little.

Thistle cocked her head to one side and considered Poppy. Then, in a matter-of-fact way, she said, "Rye's always a little weird."

"*Weird*? Why? How?"

"He gets sort of dreamy. You know, he goes off a lot by himself."

"Why . . . why do you think he ran off—this time?" Poppy wanted to know, though she had a fairly good idea.

"He's very emotional," Thistle said. "He loved Ragweed, but he sort of didn't, if you know what I mean."

"I don't think I do."

"A younger brother," Thistle whispered, as if that explained it all. Then she added, "See, Ragweed wasn't big enough to admit Rye was better than he was at some things. He was always giving Rye a hard time. And Rye, he was, well, you know, envious that his brother was everybody's favorite."

"Do you think . . . Rye . . . will come back?"

Thistle shrugged. "Yeah, sure."

Poppy tried to make herself useful by tending to the children. She was not very good at it. Besides, they were inclined to stare at her as if she were odd. Being a deer mouse she was smaller than they, and her fur was a different color.

For her own part Poppy knew perfectly well she was stalling, doing little except waiting for Rye's return. At the same time, the thought of his coming back made her nervous. She wasn't exactly sure what she felt. What would she say to him?

Poppy's thoughts were interrupted when Clover asked Valerian to bring her close.

"I need to ask you a little more about Ragweed," she said to Poppy.

"I'll tell you anything I know," Poppy said.

Clover and Valerian asked Poppy many questions. How had she met Ragweed? Where was this Dimwood Forest she had come from? Who and what was her family? Did she and Ragweed, in fact, marry?

Poppy told them all that had happened. How she had grown up with her own family on a farm at the edge of Dimwood Forest. How she had met and fallen in love with Ragweed only to be right there when the owl—a Mr. Ocax—had killed him. She told them then how she had defeated this Mr. Ocax. Finally, she told them of her desire to bring them the news of their son.

As she told her tale, she kept looking out of the corner of

her eye for Rye. The last thing she wanted was for him to show up and hear what she was saying.

"We need you to know," Valerian said, when Poppy was done, "that even though you didn't marry Ragweed we'd like to think of you as our daughter."

"We really do," Clover agreed with a catch in her voice.

"This isn't much of a home," Valerian went on, "but it's all we have. You're welcome to stay, too."

"Thank you," Poppy returned. "I'm truly touched." She reached up and took off Ragweed's earring. "I brought this back for you," she said. "It was his. I thought you should have it."

She held out the earring. The purple bead seemed to glow. The little chain sparkled.

"Did he give it to you?" Clover asked.

"In a way," Poppy said.

"Ah," Clover said softly. "He wasn't wearing one when he

left home. It must have something to do with the life he had with you."

"I have no idea where he got it," Poppy told them. "He had it on when I met him."

"Any notion what he did from the time he left here to the time he met you?" Valerian asked.

Poppy shook her head. "He never really said. But he did talk about his home fondly."

Clover held the earring in the palm of her paw, as if it were something magical. With a sigh she offered it to Valerian, who contemplated it, too.

Then Valerian handed it back to Poppy. "I think you should keep it."

Poppy looked to Clover. Clover nodded her agreement.

After a moment's hesitation, Poppy took the earring and fixed it back on her ear. "I'll stay a little while."

But Poppy knew she was only staying so she could speak to Rye. What had happened with Ragweed, she told herself, was the past. It was done. Finished. Complete. She would remember the past. But she would not live it. Instead she would wait for Rye.

But Rye did not return. Though no one seemed to be concerned, Poppy began to wonder if he would ever come back. She began to suspect—and fear—he would not.

CHAPTER 13

What Happened to Rye?

As Rye had listened to Poppy speak about Ragweed, he hardly knew what to think. He was confused. He was upset. He felt humiliated. Ragweed was always getting in his way. He had done so when he was alive. Now he was doing so even after he had died.

And yet . . .

Rye knew perfectly well that Ragweed's death *was* awful. Truly, he felt terrible about it.

And yet . . .

From the moment he had begun his dance on the meadow with this graceful mouse—this one named Poppy—he had fallen in love with her. He hoped—and thought—she felt something of the same for him. But now that she had discovered that he was Ragweed's brother—and admitted she loved Ragweed!—

surely there was no hope for *him*.

And yet . . .

He found himself thinking that perhaps, now that Ragweed had died, Poppy might turn to him.

And yet . . .

Rye felt deeply ashamed of himself. How self-centered and selfish he was! Such horrible thoughts! How low! How bad! Poppy would never be able to see anything decent in *him*.

But the very next moment he thought, "I'm not a bad mouse! I'm not!"

It was with these thoughts that Rye raced from the nest. He did not go far. He could not outrun his feelings. More importantly, he did not want to go away from this deer mouse, this Poppy.

He found himself at the edge of the beavers' pond. It was raining steadily, monotonously. The world looked the way he felt, gray and sodden. Moreover, except for him, everything seemed immense. He was nothing but a small, bad, useless mouse.

Hunkering down, consumed by the sensation that the whole world despised him, Rye shivered with wet and cold.

"Is there any place in this wide world for such a wretch as I?" he asked himself. Simultaneously, he darted a look over his shoulder to see if, just possibly, someone—he dared not say who—had followed him. When he saw that

no one had, he was angry he'd even checked.

A mournful Rye gazed down at the pond. A mist was rising off the water as if it were smoldering. A few beavers were hard at work. Suddenly Rye saw that the pond was much higher than it had been before.

Anger swept through him. How he *hated* the beavers. Yet there they were, making the dam higher, even as misery rained down on his head. Had they no feelings? Would they never stop?

As he looked on, Rye began to have an idea. If he could find some way to put an end to what the beavers were doing, might not he in some way redeem himself? Surely, if he kept them from building the dam higher, or—better yet—forced them to move away, he would become a hero to his family. He and he alone would defeat them! Why, even Poppy might see him as different from Ragweed then!

Rye surveyed the pond. The beavers' main lodge was not far from the dam. He remembered his father telling him that the way the beavers got into the lodge was by swimming through an underwater passage. If he could get into the lodge, he might . . . Actually, Rye was not at all sure what he might do. He supposed he would think of *something* once in the lodge. The main thing was to get there. Surely he could do that. Like all his brothers and sisters, he was a good swimmer.

Rye raced down to the edge of the pond.

The beavers' dam was built where the Brook had narrowed out a V in the land. The dam—made of twigs, branches, and logs plastered over with mud—was some twenty feet across and three feet wide. By going out along the dam he would be that much closer to the lodge.

But when Rye reached one end of the dam, a beaver was working on it. He had brought up a heap of mud and dumped it, and was now using his tail to smooth it down.

Though impatient, Rye bided his time. One whack of the beaver's tail—not to mention what he could do with his teeth—and Rye would be crushed.

The beaver on the dam gave some final pats to the mud, surveyed his work, uttered a few grunts, moved ponderously toward the edge of the dam, then dove into the water and swam away.

Rye crawled out upon the dam, his way impeded by the twigs and branches which were crisscrossed and bent in all directions. By the time he got near the lodge he was caked with mud and bits of leaves.

Not caring how he looked, Rye crept down as close to the water as possible. There he hesitated. Then an image of Poppy rose in his mind's eye. If he could succeed, he would be a hero. Holding his nose with one paw, Rye jumped into the water, tail first.

He landed with a splat, momentarily floundered, then righted himself. Shaking his eyes and whiskers free of water, he began to swim toward the lodge.

Three feet from the lodge, he paused and began to tread water. He had reached the most difficult part: the entrance.

Suddenly he realized he had no notion where—other than underwater—the entry hole might be. It could be on the side he was, or opposite. He would have to try his luck.

Filling his lungs with air, he let himself drop down and began to swim underwater.

It had been gray on the water's surface. It was much darker below. Before him the lodge loomed like a shadowy lump. It sat upon the bottom of the pond and rose up, a huge dome. Enormous. Impenetrable.

Stroking steadily, Rye pushed on, a trail of tiny bubbles escaping from his clenched mouth. Gradually, he began to make out what appeared to be a dark hole. Was that the entryway?

Lungs close to bursting, Rye had to make a decision. If he guessed wrong, he would drown. "At least I tried," he told himself. "Farewell, Poppy," he murmured. "Farewell, love. Farewell world!"

Kicking hard, paws madly stroking the water, he propelled himself into the hole. The moment he did so everything turned as dark as a night without a moon.

Rye was no longer trying to get into the lodge. He was struggling to save his life. His strokes were wild, his kicks frenzied.

Unable to endure any more, he shot up—and found air.

Gasping for breath, he waved his paws feebly to keep afloat and slowly moved toward a ledge of slippery mud. Reaching it, he clawed his way up, falling back a few times, finally heaving himself up on the slimy shelf. Eyes shut, he lay there, coughing and spitting water.

He opened his eyes.

He was in the lodge. A few feet away sat an enormous beaver. The beaver was looking right at him.

"Well, bless my teeth and smooth my tail," Mr. Canad said with a smile full of orange teeth. "Glad you came, pal. A stranger is just a friend you haven't met. Hey, and I mean that, sincerely."

CHAPTER 14

Ereth

Ereth ran among the trees. Heart pounding, quills rattling, he tried every dodge he knew to escape—as if some great beast were pursuing him—though this beast was his own feelings. He climbed trees. He threw himself behind bushes. It made no difference. He still felt miserable. When he found an old hollow log, he plunged into it. There, surrounded by the stench of pulpy rot and moldering fungus, he hunkered down and stared out at the rain but found no relief. Never had he felt so miserable.

Gradually the storm subsided. The rain ceased. Water dripped. A gray mist, clinging to the earth, slithered through the dark trees like forbidden thoughts.

Ereth crawled out of the log and shook himself. "Take hold of yourself," he muttered.

He headed back to the ridge in search of the cottonwood tree he had climbed when Poppy had left him. This time he found it. But when he reached it and discovered she was not there, all his desperation returned.

"Where is she?" he muttered. "Why did she leave me? What kind of friend is she, anyway? Doesn't she know I need her? She should be here helping me!"

With that Ereth wheeled about and trundled down the path he had seen Poppy take. As he came down off the crest of the ridge he saw no sign of Poppy, only the pond where beavers were hard at work.

Ereth stared balefully at the beavers. They seemed to be working nicely together. At least they were smiling at one another. "A family," he snarled with contempt. "A *happy* family."

"Crabgrass up their snoots," Ereth snapped. "I'm going back to Dimwood Forest." With that he turned, galloped up the hill, and plunged among the trees again, quickly passing through them. The next moment he burst into an open area. Before him lay a sunken meadow filled with berry brambles and flowering vines.

Paying no particular mind to where he was going, Ereth hurled himself into the most clotted part of the thicket.

It was a wild jumble, with plants growing so closely together he had to push and shove his way through the tangle of bushes. He was close to the middle when he was forced to stop. He could not move. His quills, caught in brambles and vines, held him fast. He was stuck.

Though he could not move, an exhausted Ereth was glad for the rest, glad for the quiet, glad he could not go anywhere.

"I'll stay here forever," he sighed. "Till I die. It's better that way. And it won't be long, either. Poppy was right. I'm old. Very old."

He closed his eyes and thought of home. He thought of Poppy. Momentarily, his anger rekindled. Then, grudgingly, he admitted to himself that it was he who had told her to go off by herself. Maybe her leaving him was—a little bit—his fault.

He sighed. The more he thought about her, the more he missed her. She was always so good-natured. Kind. And brave. His best friend. Perhaps he should find a way to tell her that. Someday.

With a shake of his head, he muttered, "Pickle puke," and decided it would be better not to tell her anything. It wouldn't do. She might make fun of him. Tease him. Call him that horrid word, *old*, again. Still, he might find her a seed . . . or two. He could leave them where she might find them. As if by accident. Nothing more than that. If a porcupine didn't remain prickly what could he be? *Nothing*.

Ereth settled down, relieved that it was impossible for him to do anything but stay stuck. It was better that way. Much better. He didn't have to think. Or feel . . . anything. He would just die. That, he thought, will show her!

CHAPTER 15

Rye in the Lodge

WHEN RYE HAD SWUM into the lodge he was too exhausted to offer any resistance to Mr. Canad. And by the time he did recover his strength, it was too late. The beaver had quickly constructed a cage of maple twigs and hard-packed mud, shoveled the exhausted mouse into it with his tail, then sealed the whole thing up. Rye was a prisoner.

"Well now, pal," Mr. Canad said with his usual hearti-ness, "the name is Caster P. Canad. Feel free to call me Cas. What's your name?"

Rye, wretched, gazed mournfully up at the large beaver from behind the bars of his cage. "Rye," he said.

"Absolutely delighted to meet you, pal," Mr. Canad enthused with a big grin. "Where do you live?"

"I used to live by the side of the Brook."

"Moved away, did you?"

Rye's eyes filled with angry tears. "You forced us to."

"Me? *Force* you? Not me. You could have stayed."

"We would have drowned."

"Hey, pal, that was your choice. Life isn't fair. No one promised you a rose garden. Take the good with the bad. The sweet with the sour. It all works out in the end." Mr. Canad offered another toothy smile.

"Okay," he went on, "let's cut to the chase. What made you come here?"

Rye, glowering, looked up at the enormous beaver. "To get rid of you."

"Hey, pal, you are the violent type, aren't you? You make me nervous." The beaver grinned. "Where do you live now?"

"Up by a boulder."

"A boulder? That a fact? Exactly where?"

"On the ridge. Overlooking the pond."

Mr. Canad's heart fluttered. "Not, by any chance, that boulder right on the ridge that's got a bunch of plants growing around it?"

"Yes," Rye answered.

"Well, bless my teeth and smooth my tail!" Mr. Canad glowed. "There's a piece of luck. Do you live alone?"

"With my whole family."

"Your *whole* family!" the beaver said. "Better and better. Family man myself. I love families. This is a good day."

Mr. Canad was thinking furiously: Here is a representative of that last mouse family. A violent type. He breaks in here. Okay. I'll use him to persuade them to move on their own. And it would keep my reputation for "Progress Without Pain."

"Why is it a good day?" Rye demanded, becoming alarmed. "What are you going to do to my family?"

"Hey, pal," Mr. Canad cried. "Nothing to worry about. I haven't the slightest intention of harming you or your family. You'll be as right as the rain. All tip-top. As the day is long, I'm as straight as a ruler."

Rye, staring furiously at the large beaver, said, "How can you say that when you've ruined everything?"

"Not *everything*, pal," Mr. Canad chortled. "The sun still shines, doesn't it? The moon glows? Admit it. Life goes on. We just changed a few things. Pal, when you stop looking at things selfishly—when you see the big picture—you're going to have to agree that Caster P. Canad tells it like it is.

"But for now you're going to have to excuse me while I fetch my family. We need to have a meeting to decide what to do with you." With that Mr. Canad plunged off the ledge and swam out of the lodge by way of the entry hole.

Alone and depressed, Rye sat within the cage and clutched the twig bars listlessly. He was much angrier at himself than he was at Mr. Canad. Not only had he failed to do what he set out to do, he was sure his capture would

be hard for his parents. As for Poppy, when *she* learned what he'd done, Rye had little doubt she'd think him a fool. And she'd be right. He *was* a fool.

For a while Rye tried to break the bars of his cage. He rattled them. He chewed them. But they were made of maple wood, and were too hard to cut quickly. Then he attempted digging about in the mud that held the twigs to see if that might lead to escape. That, too, proved a failure. Mr. Canad had packed it down hard. Rye had no choice but to wait and see what the beavers did with him.

He did not have long to wait. Members of the Canad family came into the lodge and examined him.

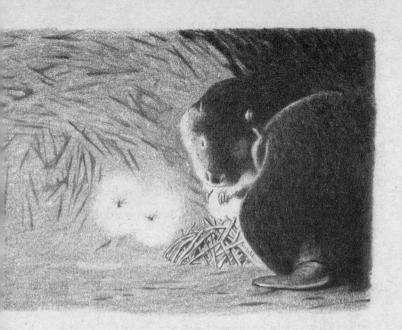

"Isn't he nasty," one said.

"What a little, puny fellow he is," another said.

"I wonder what he expected to do to us," a third said with a giggle. "He's so weak!"

Rye, sulking, shrank into a corner of his cage.

Mr. Canad, standing next to the cage, called his company to order.

"Once in a blue moon," he began, "beavers find themselves placed to do great things. But if big things are to be done, Caster P. Canad and Co. will be the one to do them."

"Hear, hear!" murmured one of the beavers.

"Way to go, Cas," said another.

"All right, then," Mr. Canad continued. "We're ready to move forward and expand Canad's Cute Condos into something grander. How about a lake?"

"Wow!"

"Fantastic!"

"Too cool!"

Beaming, Mr. Canad went on. "'Course, we'll call it Lake Canad. Here are the plans." He gestured toward the drawing on the bark.

"To make this lake, we'll need to put in a dam over by this boulder here. Turns out there's a mouse family living under that same boulder. Okay, we could just go ahead and build. They would be flooded out.

"But that's not our way, is it? Canad and Co. has a reputation for being sensitive. It's important to keep that notion afloat. We need those mice to leave on their own."

There was some beating of tails.

"Okay. How are we going to persuade these mice to move? No problem. Luck comes to those who work hard. Genius is ninety percent perspiration, ten percent inspiration. Good thing I've got the whole one hundred percent. Now, we have a visitor. A fine young mouse." Mr. Canad rapped on the cage. "Goes by the name of Rye. Rye and his family live right under the boulder we've got the old eye on."

"Keep going, Cas," one of the beavers called out, beating his tail on the ground.

"Okay. I'm going to mosey on up and have a chat with these mice. Tell them that my pal here is . . . visiting . . . with us. And," Mr. Canad added with a toothy smile, "if they want to see him again, they'd better move on. Hey!" he said, grinning, "you know what they say: Walk softly but carry a big stick in your mouth."

"You said you wouldn't hurt me!" Rye cried out.

"Easy does it, pal. Not saying I *am* going to hurt you. Remember, you broke in here. You're the violent one. I'll just warn your folks that unless they make amends by moving away, they won't ever see you again. Get it? It's their free choice. And I mean that, sincerely."

As his family applauded wildly, Mr. Canad grinned.

CHAPTER 16

Poppy Hears Some News

It was quiet in the mouse nest. In one corner Clover tended to her three youngest children. Poppy was in another corner with the older ones, including Thistle and Curleydock, telling stories about Dimwood Forest. Valerian was in the middle of the room, surrounded by children, giving them seed lessons.

"Now this kind," he was saying, holding up a plump sunflower seed, "is particularly nourishing. And tasty. You never can go wrong with sunflower seeds. Rye and I know a particularly fine place to find them." He paused and looked up and around. "Say, where is Rye?"

When none of the youngsters gave an answer, Valerian called out, "Anyone know where Rye is?"

Hearing the name, Poppy pricked up her ears and looked around, but said nothing. It was Thistle who called, "He went out."

"Do you know where?"

"Nope."

Valerian shrugged and resumed his lesson.

Poppy leaned over toward Thistle and whispered, "Do you think Rye will come back soon?"

"With Rye you never know. Poppy, please tell us some more about your forest." Thistle had grown very fond of Poppy.

Poppy talked but soon broke off. She could not concentrate. Thoughts of Rye crowded her mind. Besides, the warm, close underground air and the crowded conditions were beginning to bother her. "I think I need some fresh air," she announced.

Promising to return quickly, she made her way to the ground surface. The storm was over. Though dusk had fallen, the air had turned muggy. Poppy sat back against the boulder and looked out.

To the west a lush band of pink and purple layered the sky. Eastward a pale yellow moon had begun its climb. Fireflies punctuated the growing darkness with sparks of light, as if night itself had a bright pulse.

As Poppy remained sitting quietly, looking at nothing in particular, she thought of Ereth with a pang. She had not returned to him. Then she reminded herself how unusually grumpy he'd been. She thought, too, of his repeated statements about his preference for being alone. Poppy decided she'd stay at the mouse nest for the night. Ereth could wait.

Putting her friend out of her mind, Poppy was glad to give herself over to thoughts of Rye. She wondered where he had gone. She had little doubt as to why he'd left the nest: It was her words about Ragweed, how she had loved him and had all but married him. The distress upon Rye's face as she told the tale was as easy to see as the sun in a cloudless sky.

And yet, Poppy mused, Ragweed *was* no more. To speculate about what might have been was useless. Poppy reminded herself that she had taken this trip as a way of bringing an end to that part of her life. That had been achieved. Even as she gently touched Ragweed's earring, aware how restless she was to start life anew.

In fact, she thought with a bolt of boldness, she knew she wanted to share the rest of her life with Rye.

Sighing, Poppy looked down toward the pond. Even as she did, she saw a beaver haul himself out of the water, give himself a shake—sending a spray of water in all directions—then proceed to waddle clumsily uphill, right in her direction.

Poppy grew alarmed. She had never met a beaver before. Having heard angry accounts about them from the mice, she was not inclined to like them. She could see that, compared to her, they were enormous. Moreover, the approaching beaver's huge buck teeth—brilliant orange in color—seemed positively fierce.

Dimly she recalled that beavers and mice were related, second cousins twice removed, or something like that. At the moment she didn't *feel* related, only very small.

The beaver drew near. He had a distinct musky smell.

Poppy, not sure what to do, glanced around to make sure that, just in case the beaver meant her harm, she wasn't trapped.

When they were about four feet apart, the beaver halted.

"How you doing, sweetheart? The name is Caster P. Canad. All my friends call me Cas. As the philosopher said, a stranger is just a friend you haven't met. What's your name?"

"Poppy."

"Nice, sweetheart, very nice. You're just the one I wanted to talk to."

"*Me?*" Poppy said.

"You live under that boulder you're sitting against, don't you?"

"Well, not really," Poppy started to explain. "I've only just—"

"Hey, save your breath, sweetheart," Mr. Canad interrupted. "I know all about it. You used to live somewhere else, and you've come up here recently."

"Actually . . ." Poppy tried to interject.

"Now, unless I'm holding the stick by the wrong end—and I rarely do—there's a mouse by the name of Rye who lives here, too. Did I hit the nail on the head?"

Poppy started. "Rye? Yes, he does live here."

"Good. I like coming to the point. I play hardball and call a spade a spade."

"Is something . . . the matter with Rye?" Poppy stammered.

"Rye? The kid's as fit as a fiddle. Right as the rain. A-1 okay," Mr. Canad assured her. "Except he broke into our lodge . . ."

"Broke in!"

"Hey, I'm giving it to you straight. You heard me right. He broke in where he had no business breaking in. I mean, a beaver's lodge is his castle. That Rye is head over heels in trouble."

"Trouble!" Poppy cried, unable to do more than echo what she was hearing. "What kind?"

"Off the cuff, shooting from the hip, taking the fast lane, I'd have to say Rye is violent. But don't worry, he's perfectly safe in a cage I built in my main lodge." He pointed to one of the mounds in the pond. "Right there."

"But . . . that's awful!" said Poppy, staring at the lodge.

"You took the words right out of my mouth. He shouldn't have done it," Mr. Canad said. "Now, sweetheart, I'm talking on the up and up. We'd like to build a dam right here on this spot. Expand Canad's Cute Condos. Anchor it to that boulder. To make a long story short, it would be better for everybody if you all moved. Do it in two shakes of a beaver's tale—with no fuss—and you'll see Rye again, no worse for wear."

"But . . ."

"'Course, if you don't move . . ."

"Then what?" Poppy cried.

"Look here, sweetheart, let's just say, I don't want to beat around the bush. It's a matter of life or death. The choice is all yours. This is a free country."

"But what if . . . we don't move?" Poppy cried.

"Well, sweetheart, I'll be honest with you: I hope that doesn't happen. Because, if you don't go, I'm afraid your pal will have met his Waterloo. Sink or swim. Because your new home will be flooded, too. Some of your youngsters might drown. Naturally, that would upset my family so much—filled to the brim with anger, you know—I can't say *what* they might do to Rye. Hope I'm not boring you, but the decision is yours. Remember, we don't want to force anything on you.

"Anyway, nice talking with you, sweetheart. And have a nice day. I mean that, sincerely."

With that Mr. Canad turned and began to waddle back down toward the pond.

Poppy, finding it hard to take in all she had heard, stared after him. Her first reaction was to go racing after the beaver, tell him what she thought of him, and make him release Rye instantly. But Mr. Canad, as if knowing what Poppy was thinking, gave a great slap of his broad tail, sending out a resounding thump that shook the earth.

So instead Poppy remained where she was, watching the beaver go into the pond and swim off. Only then did she race down the entryway to Clover and Valerian's nest.

CHAPTER 17

To Help Rye

"I'VE FOUND OUT where Rye is!" Poppy shouted as she burst into the nest. "The beavers in the pond have caught him. They told me they won't let him go—or worse—unless you all move from this nest!"

The announcement brought stunned silence. It was followed by an eruption of squeaking, squealing, and talking. Clover put paws to either side of her head and cried, "It's too much!"

Valerian muttered, "I don't think I can take any more. No, I don't think I can." This seemed to give permission for the younger children to go out of control.

They raced around in circles, shouting, "It's too much. It's too much." Older children huddled in a corner and kept saying such things as, "This is so awful."

The chaos continued until Valerian, standing tall, cried, "Quiet, please."

The nest stilled.

"Poppy," Valerian said, "how do you know about this?"

Poppy repeated her conversation with Mr. Canad, concluding with the beaver's threat that if the mice did not move, Rye would remain a captive. "Or, they might do worse," she said.

Clover opened her black eyes wide. "What do you mean . . . *worse?*" she asked.

"I think the beaver was threatening to . . . harm Rye."

"Now why," Valerian cried with exasperation, "did the boy have to go off and do such a thing?"

"I bet," Thistle injected boldly, "he just wanted to show everybody he was as good as Ragweed, that's why."

Thistle's comment made Poppy look down at her toes.

"That's great," Valerian exclaimed with a rare show of anger. "If that's what he intended then he's made things worse for himself *and* us."

Valerian's words threw the nest into another uproar. Everyone was talking at once and to no particular purpose.

Clover's small, shrill voice rose above the clamor. "My dear family," she cried, "we can't take this kind of life anymore. We need to find peace. I think we'd better move out of this area entirely and start over again. Let the beavers have the Brook."

Poppy hardly knew what to say, other than to feel that in some way she was responsible for what had happened. "But," she offered timidly, "isn't there *anything* we can . . . do?"

"*Do?*" Valerian returned, eyes full of anguish. "Poppy, I tried to compromise with them. They would have none of it. Clover's right. If we're to preserve this family, we've little choice."

"I'm sorry," Poppy murmured.

"Miss Poppy," Clover said, her voice shrill with tenseness, "you've been kind enough to come here and bring us the sad news about Ragweed. Rye is our problem. Not yours. You must let us handle things our own way."

"But Clover," Poppy replied as gently as she could, "I'm not sure that even if you do leave they'll let Rye go."

"But you said that Mr. Canad promised he'd release Rye when we move," Clover cried. "What choice do we have but to trust them?"

"Clover is right," Valerian agreed. "It's the family we need to protect. There's little more to be said."

With that the mice began to scurry about, putting their possessions in order. It did not take long for Poppy to realize how much in the way, how much of an outsider, she was. Mortified, but not wishing to intrude any more than she already had, she crept from the nest.

Night had come. The moon's reflection lay upon the pond's surface like a tarnished spot of gold. Poppy could make out the islands and lodge tops, surrounded by dark water.

She thought about Rye. Just to think of him languishing in the beaver's lodge gave *her* pain. And longing. She sighed out loud.

"Don't worry," came a voice right behind her. "It's not your fault."

Poppy turned. It was Thistle. "You shouldn't take it personally," Thistle went on. "Our family has been having a bummer summer."

"I know."

The two mice sat silently side by side.

"But I bet," Thistle said after a while, "I know why Rye did it."

"Do you?" Poppy said with some hesitation. "Why?"

"Poppy," Thistle asked shyly, "did you know Rye before you came here?"

"A little. How did you know?"

"Well . . ." Thistle said, too bashful to face Poppy directly, "it was when you were talking about Ragweed. When you first came. I noticed the way you two looked at each other. Rye acted as if he was going to die. You didn't look so great, either."

Poppy turned toward the pond and gazed at the big lodge. "Then it is my fault he's where he is," she said.

"Poppy . . . ?" Thistle said.

"What?"

"You didn't make Rye do it. He went on his own. He's not your responsibility. Don't do anything weird."

"I won't," Poppy replied.

"You all right?" Thistle asked, touching Poppy gently.

"Well, yes," Poppy replied. "I just need to be alone."

"Okay," the young mouse said, and she slipped back down into the nest.

Left to herself, Poppy allowed the darkness to give her solace. Without thinking about what she was doing, she meandered down to the pond.

"If I could only tell Rye that . . ." she paused. With a jolt, Poppy recalled that she had yet to have so much as *one* conversation with the mouse. And yet, and yet, she seemed to have had so many! It was so—extraordinary!

Poppy reminded herself that she didn't *need* to be with Rye. After all, she had spent her whole life—six months— without him. Yet she *wanted* to be with him. It was hard to sort out the difference.

When she reached the water's edge, Poppy gazed out at the beaver lodges, trying to recall in exactly which one Mr. Canad had said Rye was being held. When she was sure she had located the right one she just stared at it. Knowing she was a bit closer to Rye gave her comfort. She wished she were a good swimmer.

She meandered along the shore of the pond, looking for nothing in particular but hoping some idea would come. When she came upon a splinter of wood she picked it up and balanced it in her paws. "Make a good paddle," she mused.

The moment she had *that* thought, she knew exactly what she was looking for: a piece of wood to use as a raft. With it she could float over the pond and get to Rye—somehow.

Clutching the would-be-paddle tightly, Poppy began a search. Near the stump of a chewed-down tree she found a thin, wide chip of wood. A raft.

Pushing and pulling, Poppy worked the wood chip to the water's edge, then set it afloat. The chip rode the water easily. Poppy leapt aboard. The chip wobbled but soon steadied itself. She was afloat.

CHAPTER 18

To the Lodge

Using her wood splinter as a paddle, Poppy pushed off from the shore. The raft lurched erratically until she found a way to balance it. Then, from a kneeling position, she dipped the paddle into the dark waters and began to propel herself across the pond.

Repetitious cricket sounds tickled the air. From somewhere a fox barked. A night bird called. A frog croaked. Above, the spread of stars made Poppy think of a field of bright, scattered seeds. The moon seemed to be as adrift as she.

She gazed around, trying to get her bearings, trying to recall where the main lodge was. From the middle of the pond everything seemed different.

The moonlight did allow her to make out the humps of lodges as well as islands. They seemed all alike now. She had no idea which way to go.

Poppy paddled some more, moving farther over the

pond. Knowing she had to go somewhere, she chose at random, and headed for one of the islands.

From out of the darkness she heard a splash. Coming unexpectedly, it made her jump. The next moment her raft began to rock wildly. Only by holding on tightly did she manage to keep from tumbling off.

When the waters calmed she strained to look through the darkness to determine what had caused the sound. She saw nothing. What if it were a beaver? Poppy wondered. Would it see her?

Dimly, she made out an island to her left. Its small size drew her. It would be easy to search. But after Poppy took a few more strokes, the little island seemed to have moved. Not quite believing what her eyes were telling her, Poppy stared hard. Sure enough, even as she looked, the island shifted again.

She gave a few more tentative paddle strokes. Suddenly the island moved and . . . raised its head. Poppy gasped. It was a beaver. She had almost paddled right into it.

Then to her right, there was another swell of water and a second beaver broke the pond's surface. Poppy was between them. It was the darkness that hid her.

"That you, Judy?" asked the newcomer.

"It's me," grunted the first. "Who's that?"

"Me. Joe."

"What you doing?"

"Taking a swim to cool off, the lodge is hot."

"Yeah. Hard to sleep. Hey, did you see that mouse?" Judy asked.

"The one Cas caught?" said the beaver named Joe. "I was sleeping right next to his cage. What about him?"

"What a pain," Judy said.

"If it were up to me, I'd just give him a swat with the old tail."

"Hey, you know Cas. 'Progress Without Pain.'"

"Right, sure," Joe said. "I'm going back."

"Okay."

"See you."

The beaver named Joe swam off. Poppy paddled after him as hard as she could.

Abruptly he dove beneath the water. Poppy waited and watched for him to resurface. When he didn't, she understood what had happened: The beaver must have gone into the lodge through an underwater passage.

She scrutinized the area. Sure enough, a large mound stuck out of the water nearby. She paddled until she bumped against it, then deftly leapt from her raft to the lodge. The movement inadvertently kicked the raft away. She made a grab for it, but the wood chip had already floated out of reach.

Resigned to being where she was, Poppy took a careful look around. The lodge was a mass of sticks, twigs, logs, leaves, and vines, tightly woven together and cemented with mud. It made her think of an upside-down bird's nest.

Somewhere, inside, was Rye.

Her sense of urgency renewed, Poppy returned to the water's edge and wondered if she had the courage to swim down and find the lodge's entryway. When she reminded herself what a bad swimmer she was, she began to crawl about the lodge. She had to find a way to get in.

It was at the very top of the lodge, while prying and poking amid the mud and sticks, that she discovered a hole. When she put her nose over it, she was certain she detected a flow of air—and the distinct smell of beaver—or at least of Mr. Canad. A vent hole, perhaps.

Upon examining the hole closely, she found it was big enough for her to crawl through. Perhaps it could lead her inside. Nervous, she crept in, head first. The hole was pitch black and slimy, with a sickening stench of rotting mud. It was hard to hold on.

After going down a few inches she paused. How long is this hole? she asked herself. Will I be able to get out fast if I have to? What's going to be at the end of it? Do I really want to do this? She answered herself in one word: *Rye*. She had to get to Rye.

She went on. To keep from falling, she pressed her paws tightly against the slippery sides. Down she went. It seemed endless.

As it happened, she was concentrating so hard, she came to the end of the hole without realizing she'd reached it. Catching herself just in time, she peered down into the lodge.

Such light as there was came from the occasional flashing glow of fireflies. At first Poppy thought she was looking at nothing but lumpy earth. Only gradually did she see
that right below her was a room full of sleeping beavers.
She gasped. There were so many! Some lay on their backs.
Chins up, their teeth seemed to glow like burning embers.
Some beavers were flopped over others. Others lay on
their bellies, tails occasionally flipping and flapping like
loose flags. In their restless sleep they kept shifting about,
moaning, grunting, and growling. It was as if a large mass
of mud had come seethingly alive.

From her high perch Poppy searched about for the cage
Mr. Canad had spoken of, the one in which Rye was being
held. She found it tucked away in a corner. She even
thought she saw Rye, curled up in a ball, fast asleep.

How was she going to get down to him? She dared not
jump. If she did, she'd land right in the midst of the
beavers. That was a risk she did not want to take. Then she
remembered something she'd seen on the lodge roof:
vines. Perhaps she could lower herself down. But she'd
have to work fast, before the beavers awoke.

Poppy clawed her way back to the lodge roof and
searched for a vine. When she found two twisted about a
stick she took the longest. Working fast, she tied one end
of the vine to a stick, and taking its free end in her mouth,

she crept back down the hole. When she reached the end again she lowered the vine. It dangled free. But it was impossible to see exactly how far down the vine went. Was it too far or not far enough?

Poppy could not tell.

Why was she risking her life this way? she asked herself. The same answer came as before: *Rye*.

Taking a deep breath—her heart was beating madly—she grasped the vine tightly with her front paws, wrapped her rear legs and tail about it too, and headed down the vine, headfirst.

She reached the end. It was too short. She was dangling some twelve inches over the beavers. To go any farther she would have to drop—and land on a beaver's nose. The thought of it gave Poppy the shudders.

As she tried to make up her mind what to do, Poppy's shoulders began to ache painfully. She had to either let go or go back up. She looked up. The vent hole seemed a very long way up. She looked down. The beavers seemed enormous and powerful. What would they do to her if she dropped on them?

More and more nervous, her palms grew sweaty. She shifted her grip. The shifting made the vine sway slightly. She tried to stop it but the swinging only increased. Suddenly she had an idea.

Carefully she turned about. Now she held the vine just

with her paws. Her legs and tail dangled. Poppy began to pump her rear legs hard. It made the vine sway even more. Back and forth she swung until she was moving in a great arc—like a pendulum. With every swing her heart thumped.

When Poppy reached the highest point of arc—nearest to Rye—she let go. Out she sailed through the air, right over the sleeping beavers, until she landed with a *plop* in soft mud close to Rye's cage.

There she lay, panting, heart hammering, trying to recover her breath. Had she really done it? Almost afraid to look, she lifted her head. When she saw she was beyond the beavers she took a deep sigh of relief. She turned toward the cage. There was nothing between her and it. The way was clear. Silently she crept forward and peered inside.

A firefly flashed. She saw Rye. He was curled up in a ball, fast asleep.

Poppy tried to reach through the bars to touch him. He was too far away.

"Rye!" she called softly. "Rye!"

Rye lifted a sleepy head and peered through the dark. It was by the light of a glowing firefly that he saw Poppy's face. Astonished, he squinted, unsure if what he was seeing was a dream or real.

But when Poppy said, "Oh, Rye, how glad I am to see *you*!" he knew she was the most real creature he had ever seen.

CHAPTER 19

Poppy and Rye

Poppy and Rye gazed at one another by the light of firefly flashes.

He was quite sure he was looking at the most beautiful
whiskers and pink nose he had ever seen upon any mouse
with whom he was acquainted.

Poppy was sure Rye's face, covered as it was with delicate
orange fur, was extraordinarily noble. What's more, he had
altogether splendid ears, and the small notch in the right
ear only added character.

"What," Rye said in a choked whisper, "are you doing
here?"

"I came to see if you were all right."

"But . . . why?"

"Because . . . you . . . you dance beautifully," Poppy
replied, though it made her whiskers tremble to say it.

"Thank you. And . . . you dance as if . . . as if there were
moonbeams in your toes!"

"And Rye . . ."

"What?"

"I did love Ragweed," Poppy said. "I'll never pretend I didn't. But he's . . . gone."

Rye hung his head. "I know."

"And Rye . . . you need to know. I never danced with him."

Rye looked up. His whiskers shook. "Poppy, you are the most kind, the most unselfish of mice," he whispered. "In fact, you are altogether *splendid*!"

For a moment neither spoke.

Then Poppy said, "Rye, why did you come here?"

"I wanted to do something about the beavers. To get rid of them. Somehow. Except . . . I didn't have a plan. The truth is . . . Poppy . . . I wanted to prove myself to . . . you. They caught me before I could do anything."

"Mr. Canad told me you were being held captive," Poppy said. "He said if your family didn't move, he would keep you. Forever."

"Forever," Rye repeated dramatically. "But Poppy, it will have been worth it."

"Why?"

"Because . . . you came."

"But don't you want to get out?" Poppy asked.

"I'd like to, but I think I've made things much worse."

Poppy reached her paw through the bars and touched Rye's shoulder. "That you even tried seems brave to me," she said.

"Do you truly think so?"

"Yes. Just . . . maybe . . . well, too bold."

Rye took hold of Poppy's paw—which was resting on his shoulder—and kissed it. "What you said means more . . . more . . . than a life's supply of sunflower seeds," he murmured.

They looked at one another.

Then Rye said, "How did you get in here?"

"There's a hole in the roof. I crawled down a vine."

"You *are* amazing," he said.

Poppy blushed with pleasure.

Rye became alarmed. "But how are you going to get out?" he asked.

Poppy was about to say, "The same way," but even as she had the thought, she realized it would be impossible for her to use the vine. It was dangling too high over the beavers for her to reach. "I'm not sure."

Rye said, "I swam in. Through an underwater tunnel. The way the beavers do. It's not too bad. You could go that way."

"I don't swim very well."

"Oh."

"Don't worry. I'll think of something."

Neither mouse spoke. Instead they looked at one another by the glow of fireflies.

"Rye," Poppy said, suddenly becoming more brusque as she felt the urgency to leave, "have you tried chewing through these bars?"

"They're too tough."

Poppy tried for herself. She gave up quickly. "I see what you mean."

"I'm afraid," Rye said, "I really am going to stay here forever. . . . I suppose I'll die of old age and . . . regret."

"Rye . . ."

"What?"

"Please, I know the bars are tough, but keep chewing on

them. I'll find a way back to your family nest. They need to know you're all right. And maybe if I get a longer vine, one that reaches the ground, we could get you out that way."

"Do . . . do you think so?"

"Maybe." She started to back away.

Rye, clinging to the twig bars, called, "Poppy!"

"What?"

"I'm deeply moved that you came. But . . . maybe you shouldn't return. I don't want you to risk your life . . . for me."

"But Rye . . ." she said, taking a few more steps toward the cage.

"What?"

"I would . . . I would like to dance again."

"Oh, Poppy," Rye cried out. "So would I! With you!"

"*Shhh!*" Poppy cautioned as she backed away. Unable to take her eyes from Rye, she stumbled over a sleeping beaver's tail.

She stood still. Rye, looking on, was horrified. For a long moment, they dared not move. Finally, the beaver rolled away, then settled down, never having awakened.

Poppy crept over to the far wall. The way was muddy. By pressing up against the wall she was able to skirt a large, sleeping beaver and come around to the edge of the water gate.

Once there she gazed into the murky water apprehensively, then looked around to see if there was any way to get up to the vine. It was impossible. She had no choice. Reluctantly she turned back to the water. The prospect of swimming caused her so much dread, she felt compelled to give herself a reassuring hug. Taking a deep breath, she jumped, hitting the water with a splash.

Across the lodge Mr. Canad sat up and looked around. He had heard something. Taking a few sniffs, he detected a vague and unusual smell. He peered about but saw nothing except bulky beavers sleeping. All seemed perfectly normal. And yet—what was it he had heard?

He sniffed again. That time he detected the faint smell of . . . *mouse*. Could the mouse have escaped?

"Better safe than sorry," Mr. Canad allowed and got up. Approaching Rye's cage, he peered through the gloom. At first he couldn't see Rye, but by listening intently, he heard the sound of chewing.

He crept closer to the cage. Rye was at the back of the cage, gnawing on a bar.

Mr. Canad broke into a toothy smile. "Well, bless my teeth and smooth my tail," he snorted. "You're trying to be a beaver!"

Rye, taken by surprise, looked up.

"Don't think you should try chewing your way out, pal,"

Mr. Canad said. "We need you to stay."

Glowering, Rye said nothing.

"Just back away from those bars, pal. You don't want to cross over the line and force my paw. If I do something bad, it'll be your own fault."

Rye stepped away.

"Way to go, pal. Now, look," Mr. Canad went on to say, "I think I'll catch my Zs here. For the next few days, anyway. Don't want to lock the barn door after the horses are gone."

Mr. Canad was about to settle himself when he recalled the noise that had woken him. If this mouse was here, what was *that* sound? Now that he thought about it . . . could it have been a . . . splash?

He sat up and counted his beavers. All present and accounted for.

He did an inspection around the cage area. In the mud were Poppy's prints.

"You've had a visitor!" the beaver suddenly exclaimed. "Haven't you?"

"Leave me alone!" Rye cried.

"Never mind," said Mr. Canad. "One picture is worth a thousand words. One of your pals was here."

The beaver scrutinized the lodge intently. By a firefly flash he caught sight of the vine dangling from the lodge roof. Mr. Canad grunted. "The vent hole."

He lumbered across the lodge floor and ripped the vine down. "Better plaster some mud over that hole," he thought. "I can always make some other holes—and hide them. Don't want any mice in the ointment."

CHAPTER 20

Poppy

THE COLDNESS OF THE WATER—its utter darkness—shocked Poppy. Not only did she not move, she didn't know which way *to* move. Instead, she sank, spiraling down. Unless she did something quickly, she would drown.

She began to thrash wildly. Her frenzy got her nowhere. Still sinking, she tried to think herself into calmness, succeeding just enough to move her legs and arms in unison. Within moments she bumped against some twigs. She grabbed hold.

Her breath was giving out. Letting go of the twigs, she clawed frantically upward and forward, hoping she was clear of the lodge.

Like a cork popping from a bottle, Poppy burst upon the pond's surface. Splashing frantically, she gulped great drafts of air into her hungry lungs.

She looked up. Through water-logged eyes she saw blurry bits of light. At first she thought they were fireflies.

Then she realized she was seeing stars. Never before had stars seemed so beautiful. She was out of the lodge.

Now, however, she had to get to the shore. She doubted her ability to swim. Flailing, she tried to make some sense of where she was. She did see what appeared to be other lodges. She wanted to avoid them.

As she floundered, she felt a bump on her head. Ready to defend herself, she whirled. It was only a chip of wood. Eagerly, she held on. It kept her afloat.

Clinging to the chip, Poppy kicked vigorously. She began to move forward.

Her progress was slow. Her energy was ebbing. Now and again she rested her head on the wood chip. She forced herself to think of Rye, caged in the beaver's lodge. "At least I'm free," she chided herself and resumed kicking.

Twenty minutes later she came to a lurching halt. In a daze she looked up. Land rose before her. She had reached the shore.

A weary Poppy stumbled out of the water. Once on land she gave herself a vigorous shake, ridding herself of what felt like a ton of water. Much lighter, she lay down on the ground and cradled her head in her paws. Only then did she allow herself to feel the full depth of her exhaustion. Never again, she vowed, would she go into water.

As she lay there she thought of the imprisoned Rye and

reviewed her plan. She would get another vine—longer than the one she had just used—and drop it down the vent hole. She would go down again, and somehow get Rye out of the cage. Then the two of them would climb out. There was no other way. And she wanted it to happen quickly.

Poppy hurried up the hill.

By the time she reached the boulder, the pink glow of sunlight had begun to bloom upon the eastern horizon. Birds began to twitter madly. It was as if a night of silence had been too much to bear, and there was a desperate need to make up for lost time.

She considered the pond. As Poppy watched, a swarm of beavers emerged from the lodge where she knew Rye was being held. She studied them with intense anger. They were so large and powerful. And those teeth and huge tails . . .

She hurried into the nest.

The mice were astir, but moving about as though weighted by great burdens. No one looked up or around. Talk was minimal. Little tasks were being performed with minute attention. The family was preparing to move.

"I'm back," Poppy announced.

The mice paused in their work and looked around.

"Ah, Poppy," Valerian said sadly, "I thought you had left us."

"Not at all. I went to see Rye."

"Rye!"

"How'd you do that?" Curleydock called out.

Poppy told how she got into the beavers' lodge, and of her subsequent visit with Rye. "He's not happy," she told them, "but he's all right."

"But . . . why did he even go there?" Clover asked.

"He wanted to do something about the beavers."

"Did he?"

"No."

Valerian's tail waved in agitation. "Why that mouse must always be trying to prove himself I can't begin to imagine. And now, a prisoner, held for a ransom, the ransom being our moving away. Well, we're trying to go as quickly as we can."

"I do have a plan to free him," Poppy offered.

The nest became very still.

"Miss Poppy," Valerian said, drawing himself up and speaking somberly, "ever since you came to our nest, you've been telling and doing some remarkable things. We don't doubt you are an exceptional creature. Perhaps living quietly and simply by the Brook, we've become a tad shy of difficulty. No doubt the beavers have unnerved us, too. But the truth is," Valerian concluded, "it would be better if we just gave in."

"Won't you even listen to my plan?"

Valerian sighed. "I guess we can. You just mustn't expect us to do anything."

As Rye's family stared at her with dull eyes and twitching ears, an uncomfortable Poppy stood in the middle of the nest. She felt some anger. These mice had been generous when she told them of Ragweed's death. Now that she was suggesting they *do* something to keep Rye from dying, they were not so hospitable.

"I got into the beavers' main lodge," she told them anew, "by using a vent hole and a vine to drop down inside. Unfortunately, Rye and I couldn't break his cage. I need more teeth or paws. I'll need a few of you to join me when I return to the lodge with a longer vine."

"Go into the beavers' lodge?" cried an alarmed mouse.

"Right. The way I did."

"Wouldn't that be dangerous?" called another. "Those beavers are so big. A swat of their tails—"

"And what about those teeth . . ." still another said. "One bite and . . . good-bye."

Poppy held up a paw to still the objections. "I have a friend. My best friend. He came with me here from Dimwood Forest."

"Another mouse?" asked one of the youngsters.

"He's a porcupine. His name is Ereth. Porcupine quills

are very sharp. My friend is always losing his. I'll get some. When we go into the lodge we'll each carry a quill to defend ourselves."

"One quill against all those *beavers*?" asked another.

"Exactly."

"Where is this friend of yours?" someone asked.

"Waiting for me up beyond the ridge."

Valerian cleared his throat. "Poppy, how many of us do you propose it will take to get Rye out?"

"There's me, of course," she replied. "But I'll need at least a couple of others."

No one spoke.

It was Clover who said, "Poppy, perhaps you could get Rye out. But what about the beavers? They'll simply go on building. What will happen to the rest of us?"

"I'm not sure," Poppy admitted. "But I must free Rye."

"My dear," Clover said, "I do wish I could believe your plan would be helpful. I truly do. But, no, I . . . can't." She turned to Valerian. "Do you?" she asked.

Valerian gazed at his feet. "It seems awful risky," he said gloomily. He looked up. "And it sure will create greater danger for the rest of us."

No one spoke. Then, speaking gently, Poppy said, "But, as I understand it, you've not resisted them at all."

Once again there was silence.

Valerian cleared his throat. "Poppy," he said, "since this matter concerns the family I think we need to talk this over. Privately."

"All right," Poppy said, trying to hide her disappointment. "I'll go where my friend is waiting, gather up some quills, and bring them back. When I do, you can tell me what you'd like to do."

"I think that would be best," Valerian agreed.

An angry Poppy ran up the entryway, took one more look down at the pond and the lodge where she knew Rye was being kept, then hurried up toward the ridge.

She had no trouble finding the cottonwood where she had seen Ereth go. But the porcupine was nowhere in sight.

CHAPTER 21

Ereth Has More Thoughts

DEEP WITHIN THE THICKET, unable to move, Ereth was thinking hard:

"I probably shouldn't be so hard on Poppy. She's only a mouse. Small. Helpless. Talks a lot. Jabbers. Too cheerful most of the time. Nothing but squirrel sludge and buzzard belch.

"But then, she doesn't know the world. Not like I do. She needs protecting. Actually, there's no one around who can protect her better than me. I've done it before. I could do it again. I know the world. Know how it works. Not that she appreciates me. What was it she said about me . . . *old*.

"I'm not old. Maybe I *look* old . . . but inside, where it counts . . . I'm young. Young as her. Younger! I'm good-looking too— in my way. Fine set of quills. And I'm smart. Very smart.

"I wonder what she thinks of me. Really thinks. Wonder if she likes me. Really likes me. The way I . . . like . . . her. I suppose, in a way, I do like her. A lot. I can . . . allow that.

"Point is, I could do a lot for her. More than she could guess. Show her the world. Teach her the way it works.

"Now, with her being off on her own I'm always worried about her. But with me around, she'd never be in danger.

"I wonder if—just suppose—if she would, well . . . all she ever talks about is . . . love . . . and that Ragweed. What did he know about love? Or her for that matter. She told me he loved her. *Love*. Young folk think they're the only ones who love. Phooey! Nothing but slug splat stew and weasel jam.

"Still, if she wanted me to—as a favor—I could love her. She'd probably like that. If she'd give me the chance.

"Wonder what she'd say if I hinted at it. Or suggest it. I mean, maybe I could say—I . . . love you—well, once. Not too loudly. A little bit. Just so she knew. I wouldn't have to say it again.

"She'd like that. Then we could get married. There would be talk. She being young. Me . . . older. We wouldn't care. Not us. She's got a mind of her own. So do I.

"I bet she'll be thrilled. I'm big. Powerful. Smart. Could give her lots of advice. She's a good listener. And it'll be good to have someone young around that old smelly log of mine. She could clean it up. A bit. A small bit. Not too much. Yes, she'd like it. Yes, soon as I see her again, I'll tell her. Sort of. Some way . . ."

So ran Ereth's thoughts, stuck as he was, deep within the thicket.

CHAPTER 22

Poppy Makes Up Her Mind

THOUGH POPPY WAITED at the tree, Ereth did not return. Knowing how unpredictable her friend was, she kept asking herself how long she should wait. After all, she had been with the mice longer than she'd planned. That certainly would have irritated the old porcupine.

She began to think he'd done what he'd threatened to do all along—trundled back to Dimwood Forest. Yet Poppy was quite aware her friend might be doing no more than taking a nap in a nearby log.

Normally, Poppy would not have minded waiting. But she kept worrying that if she were going to save Rye, she had to act swiftly.

Having nothing better to do, she searched about the base of the cottonwood tree for some of Ereth's quills to take back to the nest. When she failed to find any, she became fretful. The thought of sneaking into the beavers' lodge without the protection of quills was something she did not relish.

Having no quills set off a nervous train of doubts in Poppy's mind. Would she be able to get into the lodge again? Was Rye's cage breakable? What if she or he got hurt? Would they be able to use the vine to get out of the lodge? And what if freeing Rye *did* bring greater harm to the rest of his family? Maybe Valerian and Clover were right. Maybe it all *was* too dangerous.

The more Poppy thought, the more doubts she had about her plan.

Suddenly Poppy felt an intense desire to race back to Dimwood Forest and hide. There she would be safe and secure in the world she knew and loved best. It was bittersweet to recall that when she had begun this trip, she had been looking forward to a time of calm. Perhaps Ereth was right. Perhaps it was better to be alone.

And yet she had fallen in love with Rye. Moreover, she had promised to help him. How could she abandon him? She could not, no more than she could abandon her feelings.

Too agitated to wait any longer for Ereth, Poppy hurried down the hill and crept back into the nest. It was very crowded. Some fifty and more mice were there, most of whom she had not seen before.

She caught hold of Thistle. "What's happening?" Poppy asked.

"It's the rest of our family," Thistle explained. "Valerian asked them to come hear about your plan."

"Are they for it or against it?" Poppy asked.

"They can't make up their minds," Thistle confided. "Poppy, I think we should do it—as long as we have quills to defend ourselves."

"Thistle," Poppy confided, "I couldn't get the quills."

Thistle blanched. "You couldn't?"

"My friend, the porcupine, has disappeared."

"Does that mean we can't rescue Rye?" Thistle asked with dismay.

Poppy, feeling she had failed the young mouse, hardly knew what to say. "I'm not sure," she replied.

Valerian approached. "Poppy, I sent word to the rest of

the family about what you want to do," he informed her. "It's so important I felt everyone should be involved in the decision.

"Attention, please!" he cried.

The mice hushed.

"For those who don't know her yet," Valerian said by way of introduction, "this is Poppy. She comes to us from out east. She was a special friend of Ragweed's. That makes her a good friend of ours."

To this there were murmurs of assent.

"You've heard what's happened to Rye and what choice we've been given," Valerian continued. "Move off somewhere—and, hopefully, have Rye freed—or try to save Rye on our own, and take our chances with the beavers.

"To be honest with you, your mother and I think it'd be best to move on. Poppy here wants to rescue Rye. Since

this concerns the whole family, we thought it'd be wise for you to hear her for yourselves."

Once again Poppy found herself facing a world of grave, golden faces. Momentarily she thought of sharing her anxieties, but feared that if the mice knew how nervous she was, they would never give her help. Instead, she simply explained her plan for freeing Rye.

"Did you get those quills?" someone asked when she was done.

"I'm afraid not."

A nervous twitter passed over the family.

"I do need some volunteers," Poppy said, almost timidly.

Curleydock shyly lifted a paw. "I'll . . . go," he offered.

"Me, too," Thistle joined in.

"What about the rest of you?" Poppy asked. "Can I have your approval?"

Valerian cleared his throat. "Poppy, if you don't mind waiting outside, I think it would be easier for us to make up our minds."

It was a discouraged Poppy who left the nest.

Once above ground she gazed down at the pond and the lodge where she knew Rye was being kept. "Think of it," she told herself, "as just another kind of dance."

Thistle and Curleydock emerged from the nest.

Poppy looked at them expectantly.

Thistle said, "They think you're making a mistake, but they won't keep you from trying. They're going to move. So we're on our own."

Poppy considered her young friends. "Please," she said to them, "you're very brave to volunteer. But it will be hard. Maybe impossible. I won't think less of you if you change your minds."

"No way," Thistle said with a stubbornness that made Poppy recall Ragweed. "We're going with you."

Curleydock nodded in agreement.

"All right then," Poppy said briskly as she tried to stir up her own energy. "The first thing we need to do is get a long piece of vine. Any idea where we can get one?"

The young mice exchanged looks. "Maybe up by the berry thicket," Curleydock suggested.

With Curleydock leading the way, the three mice scampered up the hill. A short run brought them up and over the ridge. On the far side they went down into a sunny hollow. Before them lay an overgrown thicket of berry bushes and flowering honeysuckle vines. The air was filled with sweetness.

"We should be able to get a honeysuckle vine there," Thistle said. "They're long and tough."

The three mice were soon deep within the thicket. Cool and moist, it was perfumed by the almost overpowering, sticky-sweet scent of berries.

"How about this vine?" Curleydock asked. He was yank-ing on a green strand that twisted high over their heads and out of sight.

"It really needs to be long and strong," Poppy urged. "It has to get us into the lodge and out."

"This one looks okay," Thistle called from another spot. She was joined by the others.

"Haul it in," Poppy said. While the other two worked to untangle the vine, she chewed through its roots. Then they began to pull.

"It's stuck," Thistle announced.

"Must be tied around something," Curleydock agreed.

No matter how hard the three pulled, the vine would not come.

"We can follow it along," Poppy suggested.

Curleydock was up front. Thistle was in the middle. Poppy came behind. As they followed the vine they became increasingly spread out, losing sight of one another.

Suddenly, from deep within the thicket, there was a fran-tic call from Curleydock. "Help!" he cried. "Hurry! Fast!"

Poppy and Thistle dropped the vine and charged for-ward. Curleydock was crouched down in terror.

Looming over him was Ereth.

"Ereth!" Poppy cried.

"Poppy," Ereth snapped, "you simple smudge of a slimy slug! Where have you been?"

Poppy grinned. "I've been busy. But I've been looking for you. What are you doing here?"

"Never mind. Just get me out of here. I'm stuck." He pulled back and forth but his quills continued to hold him fast.

"Ereth," Poppy said, "this is Thistle and Curleydock. They're brother and sister to Ragweed."

"Ragweed," Ereth said. "I'm sick of talk about Ragweed. Just get me out. I need to talk to you."

"What about?"

"Just get me out!"

Poppy turned to Curleydock and Thistle. They had been looking on in great puzzlement. "It's all right," she told them. "He's perfectly harmless."

"Bee butter!" Ereth roared. "I am not harmless! I have a terrible temper. I say dreadful things. I'm a selfish old coot who does what he wants when he wants and doesn't care what anyone else wants."

"He's really good," Poppy said.

"Don't listen to her. I'm bad!" Ereth screamed.

Nonetheless the three mice set to work chewing away at the vines that had ensnared Ereth. Even as they did, the impatient porcupine tossed and pulled, trying to free himself. Finally, with a snap, he broke loose.

"Now," Ereth said, "tell those friends of yours to beat it. I have something important to tell you."

"I'm sure they could listen—"

"It's private, mush-head!"

Poppy looked to Thistle and Curleydock, who, understanding, scampered off.

"I've got something to tell you, too," Poppy said when they were gone.

"You have to listen to me first," Ereth insisted. "What I've been thinking is . . ." He stopped, suddenly bashful and tongue-tied.

"What is it?"

"It's just that . . . what I think is . . . Now, see here, Poppy . . . I . . . wish . . . I wish . . . I had a piece of salt! Tell me what you wanted to say first."

"Are you sure?"

"Push the barf button and take a bath! I just said so, didn't I?"

"Well, then," said Poppy, blushing with pleasure. "Ereth . . . I've fallen in love."

"You . . . *what?*" Ereth whispered, aghast.

"Fallen in love."

"With . . . whom?" Ereth asked. He was trembling with emotion.

Poppy smiled. "I know it must seem strange, but you see,

I met . . . well, actually, he's Ragweed's brother. His name is Rye and he's . . . But what's the matter?"

"Thief! Crook!" Ereth yelled. "I'll skewer him! Whack him! Mash him! Turn him into skunk gunk."

"Ereth! What are you talking about?"

"You just think I'm too old," the porcupine ranted, rearing up and down as though bitten by ants. "Too stupid! Too big. Too sour. Too . . . me!" Abruptly he whirled around and began to rush away.

"But that's not true," Poppy called after him. "It's not. And what did you want to tell me?"

"Forget it," Ereth called back. "I'm leaving."

"Where are you going?"

"To Dimwood Forest, pickle seed!" he cried.

"Ereth!" Poppy called after him. "Please don't go. I need you!"

"You're on your own, traitor!" the porcupine shouted as he tore from view.

With great puzzlement Poppy gazed after him. Something was surely the matter with her friend. With a sigh, she wished she understood him better.

She glanced around. To her great relief she saw that in his fury Ereth had dropped some quills. She gathered them up and hurried to find Thistle and Curleydock.

CHAPTER 23

The Rescue Begins

"How do we get to the lodge?" Curleydock asked after Poppy had given him and Thistle a lesson in the use of the quills. "We can swim. Can you?"

"Not really," Poppy admitted. "When I went to the lodge before I floated on a wood chip."

"The beavers leave all kinds of chips around," Thistle said. "I'm sure we could find one big enough to carry the three of us."

The trio crept down to the edge of the pond. A few beavers were about, working.

"Don't let them see us," Poppy warned.

Squatting down, the mice attempted to hide behind bushes. Only when Poppy was sure they were unnoticed did she and the others scout about in search of a chip.

Thistle found one near a recently chewed stump. All agreed the thin, square flake would be large enough to carry the three of them.

Quickly, they dragged it behind a bush and hid it, then searched out wood bits to use as paddles. Then they returned to the top of the hill.

"Better get some rest," Poppy suggested. "As soon as it gets dark we'll go."

As far as she was concerned all was ready.

But the mice *had* been observed. Clara Canad saw them sniffing about the edges of the pond. Suspicious, she had watched intently, but was not certain what the mice were doing.

She reported what she'd seen to Mr. Canad. "What do you think?" she asked him.

"Don't know," he replied. "Don't want to make a mountain out of a mouse hill. Still, you might have a point. Give them an inch, these mice take a mile."

"The mice I saw were looking for something."

"What do you think it was?" Mr. Canad asked.

"I'm not sure. Did you block that vent hole?"

"Piece of cake."

"Did you make another?"

"Needle in a haystack. But look here, sweetheart, the less trouble, the better. We've been coasting along easy. We don't want to slip on banana peels now. So if you want to keep on watch, far as I'm concerned, that's frosting on the cake."

With that, Mr. Canad swam away.

"Well, I don't like it," Clara said to herself. "I'm going to patrol the pond tonight."

The farewells Thistle and Curleydock made to their family that night were brief and painful. The elder mice tried to be kind but could do little to hide their apprehension. For their part the youngsters tried to appear bold, but felt only uneasy.

Poppy, uncomfortable with the family's disapproval, kept away entirely.

It was dark when the three mice went down to the pond. The vine hung in a coil around Poppy's neck like a life preserver.

Once they located the wood chip they had hidden, they pushed it into the water, then jumped on. In moments they were afloat, moving slowly toward the lodge.

The three mice knelt on the wood chip and paddled steadily. Thistle and Curleydock were up front. Poppy was in the rear. Now and again she stood tall and peered into the dark, trying to keep them on course. The beavers' main lodge, though visible, was distant. "To the left," she called. "To the right." Thistle and Curleydock shifted their paddles accordingly.

Other than normal night sounds, all was quiet. The moon kept slipping in and out behind clouds. A breeze from the north had begun to blow, bringing early hints of the autumn yet to come. It made the pond surface choppy.

Thistle's whispered voice broke through the dark. "I think I heard something."

The mice stopped paddling. Poppy's ears twitched. She was not sure, but she too had caught a faint, splashing sound off to her left. The noise, however, did not return.

"I think we're all right," she called, keeping her voice low. The three resumed their paddling.

As they approached the lodge, Curleydock whispered, "Is that it?"

"I'm pretty sure," Poppy replied.

"Which side should we aim for?" Thistle wanted to know.

"It doesn't matter," Poppy said. "We'll be crawling to the vent hole on top. Let's go. Keep your voices low."

They dipped their paddles and moved forward again. Even as they did, a great swell of water lifted their raft, causing it to slide back as if it were rolling down a hill.

The next moment, Clara Canad, orange teeth glowing, rose up before them.

"I thought I heard something," she barked. "What are you doing here? What are you trying to do?"

"Back paddle!" Poppy yelled frantically and plunged her oar deep into the water as if she could scoop them clear.

Thistle tried, too, but with no more success. Worse, when she hauled back the strain was so great her paddle snapped in two. Curleydock, working frantically, only stirred the foaming waters.

With the raft rocking wildly, Thistle slipped. She did manage to hang on by the tips of her paws, but her hold was precarious. Curleydock, seeing her danger, attempted to reach for her, but lost his step on the listing raft and flipped over her head into the water.

"Curleydock!" Thistle screamed. She twisted to see where he had gone. He had vanished.

Clara, meanwhile, swung herself completely around, and lifted her tail.

"Look out!" Poppy cried.

Poppy saw Thistle attempt to draw her quill. It caused her to lose her grip. She fell back into the water and disappeared.

As the beaver's tail struck, Poppy clung to the raft. The tail hit the raft's front end, causing it to flip up and over like a catapult, flinging Poppy into the air.

As she flew she spread her legs wide, landing in the water on her belly with a splat. Stunned, she lay facedown in the water. It was the vine, still around her neck, which kept her from drowning.

Clara looked around. Seeing Poppy facedown in the water, she assumed she was dead. As for the other two mice, she did not see them at all. She was sure they, too, had perished.

With a satisfied grunt, the beaver dove beneath the water and headed for the entryway to the lodge.

Poppy, regaining consciousness, looked up. Giving her head a shake, she spat out water and called, "Thistle! Curleydock!" Her voice was weak. There was no reply.

She looked about. The beaver's lodge rose up before her. Giving a few feeble kicks, she moved close enough to reach out and grab hold of some of its branches. When she pulled at them, she came up against it. There she rested some more until her wind was completely restored. Only

then did she crawl out of the water and onto the lodge. Turning, she gazed back over the pond.

"Thistle!" she called again. "Curleydock!"

She thought she heard an answering cry, but when it did not repeat itself, she was sure her young friends had drowned.

Drenched and forlorn, Poppy sat down, toying with the circle of vine by her side. Suddenly, she reached for her quill. It, too, was gone. That meant she had no way to defend herself. Everything bad that could have happened, had.

What she should do, she told herself, was to go back and inform Valerian and Clover what had occurred. The mere thought of it made her groan. Why did she always have to bring bad news? It was all too ghastly.

The next moment she realized that going back was not possible. Her raft was gone. She couldn't swim to shore. There was little choice but to press on and attempt to save Rye—somehow.

Poppy hefted the circle of vine. Though heavy, she flung it back over her neck, then began to climb the side of the lodge.

As she went she began to cry. Why did Ragweed have to die? Why did Rye have to run away? Why did Ereth and Clover and Valerian have to be angry at her? Why did Thistle and Curleydock have to drown? Was everything her fault? It was all too much.

Despite her anguish, Poppy continued up the side of the lodge. It was a hard climb. Her own distress, the rough nature of the lodge's construction, her sense of failure, all conspired to make the going difficult. Even so she kept climbing constantly, slipping, banging her head, her knees. Her paws grew raw. More than once she had to stop and regain her breath as well as her composure. But up she went, crawling on, over, under, and around twigs, sticks, and logs, all the while slipping and sliding over mud that stuck to her like glue. Sometimes the agony of it all made her whimper.

And then, when she finally reached the top, she could not find the vent hole. She could hardly believe it. Back and forth over the top she crawled. All she found was mud and more mud. Something was wrong, altered.

Gradually, Poppy began to grasp what must have happened. When she had visited Rye she had left the vine dangling from the vent hole. The beavers must have discovered what she'd done and covered the hole with mud. If that was true—and it certainly seemed to be so—then, short of swimming, there was no way for her to get into the lodge.

Feeling defeated and alone, Poppy sat atop the lodge. Ereth had fled back to Dimwood. Thistle and Curleydock were gone, presumably drowned. Rye was imprisoned. Rye! How close he was. How impossible to reach! Her whole plan was a disaster.

Poppy lay back and stared up at the few stars peeking out now and again from behind drifting clouds. I might as well be up there for all I can do, she thought.

Exhaustion—fueled by sorrow and defeat—took hold. She kept telling herself she mustn't sleep, that she must do something. But her fatigue, mixed with her melancholy state, proved too powerful. She nodded off.

CHAPTER 24

Valerian and Clover

THOUGH THE PACKING of the nest had been completed, Valerian and Clover decided to wait for the morning to make their move. Without saying so, both were reluctant to go farther away from Rye, Thistle, and Curleydock. In any case, it was night and the children were asleep. Better not to disturb them.

Sitting side by side, paw in paw, the two mice stared up at the moon, which kept slipping behind the scudding clouds. Lifting their noses and sniffing at the breeze, they listened to the hum and buzz of the night. Sometimes they gazed down toward the pond and the lodge where they knew Rye was being held.

"I wonder where Poppy and those kids are now," Valerian mused.

"I just hope they're all right," Clover said.

"That Poppy is a tough one, love," Valerian said, trying to sound more reassuring than he felt. "I didn't think going was a good idea, but if anyone can get Rye out and come back safe, I suppose she can."

"And here we sit," she said.

Valerian nodded.

Suddenly Clover sighed. "Oh, Valerian," she whispered, "when I saw the faces of the family, it made me think how much I love them all. It isn't wrong to want to protect them, is it?"

"I don't think so," Valerian replied kindly. "I feel that way myself."

For a moment they were quiet.

Then Clover sighed. "Valerian, how long have we been together?" she asked.

"Six years."

"Such a long time," Clover said. "And a good time. A good life. So many children. Good children. Mostly. They come. They go. And here we are. Sometimes, Valerian, it seems the only difference with us is that you're grayer, I'm fatter, and we're both a lot more tired."

"You're still my love, Clover," Valerian murmured, giving her paw a gentle squeeze.

"Valerian . . ." Clover said, as if she hadn't heard, "I suppose sometimes it takes an outsider to see what we can't see for ourselves. I've been thinking about what Poppy said. What she said is true: I haven't put up much resistance to the beavers. I've been too . . . fearful that some of us would get hurt . . . or worse. But sitting here, with you, looking on, I . . ."

She faltered, took a deep breath. With a painful catch in her throat, she said, "Valerian . . . Poppy was right. We can't just accept what these beavers are doing to us. It'll only get worse. Valerian, I just wish we could do something. *Anything.*"

Having spoken, Clover buried her face in Valerian's shoulder and began to weep.

Valerian patted her gently. Then he said, "Well, love, what do you have in mind?"

"That's just it," she whispered between sobs. "I don't know. But why," she cried, "did those beavers have to build that dam?" She hid her face again.

Valerian gazed down at the dam. Then he shifted about, looked at the boulder, then down at the dam, then the boulder again. "Maybe . . ." he said softly, "what we should do is . . . bust it."

Taken aback, Clover looked up. "*Bust their dam?*" she cried in astonishment.

"Look here," Valerian continued. "Maybe we had no right to say they couldn't come here and build. It wasn't our brook. But they've taken over. Taken everything. If we busted that dam," Valerian continued, "the pond water would drain away. All the animals could use the Brook again. The way we did before."

"But we're *mice*, Valerian!" Clover squeaked. "We're small. It's huge. They're huge. How could we do anything big like that?"

Valerian looked all around. Then, nodding, he said, "I'll tell you how . . . by using the boulder we've been living under. Always seemed to me it might topple on its own. Well, listen here, love, suppose we dig around it and under it. Get it loose. Then, well, give it a shove. Let it roll down the hill so that it hits the beavers' dam smack on. I bet you a pile of acorns it'd punch out a pretty big hole. Water would drain right out."

"But . . ." Clover said, quite flabbergasted, "how could you get it to go the right way?"

Valerian studied the boulder, the hill, then the pond anew. "Let's say we made a kind of ditch right in front of it. Sort of a chute. Of course, we'd have to aim it right at the dam. If we did it properly it couldn't miss."

Clover stared at her husband with wide-eyed admiration. "Valerian, do . . . do you think we really could do that?"

Valerian was getting more and more excited. "We've got the whole family around, don't we? If everybody pitched in, worked hard, I think we could do it. But we'd have to do it right away. By dawn. Once we start, those beavers will figure out what we're doing."

"I'd want to work, too," Clover assured him. "One of us could be in charge of digging around the boulder. The other could make that ditch."

"Right!" Valerian cried. "But, like I said, we better do it right away."

"But what about Rye, Thistle, and Curleydock? And Poppy?"

"Can't see where it'd do them any harm. Might even make things easier for them. And if it works, maybe the beavers will go away," he added, with new determination in his voice. "Forever."

Clover looked at him. Suddenly she cried, "Oh, Valerian, I'm so glad it's you I love. I truly am!" And she threw her paws about him and gave him a tight hug, which he returned.

The next moment the

two went rushing down into their nest. "Everybody up! Everybody up! There's work to do!"

The family having been roused, Valerian and Clover told them of the plan. Sensing their parents' enthusiasm, all the children pitched in eagerly.

In quick time, under Clover's direction, some thirty golden mice were scraping the earth away from around the boulder. Though their paws were small and could carry but little at a time, they attacked the task with great determination. The dirt began to fly.

Simultaneously, directly in front of the boulder and aimed right at the dam, Valerian and his crew marked out the ditch.

Valerian had but one worry: Could they do it all fast enough?

CHAPTER 25

Inside the Lodge

ATOP THE BEAVERS' lodge, Poppy woke with a start. How long had she slept? She stood tall and looked east. There was a faint hint of dawn. It made her heart lurch. With the coming of dawn she was sure the beavers would awaken. When they did, she would lose whatever chance she had to free Rye. A great deal of time already had been lost.

She scrambled to the top of the lodge where she thought the vent hole had been. As before, all she found was mud. This time, however, she was desperate. Putting the vine ring aside, she clawed at the mud. While heavy and thick, it was capable of being dug. Poppy began to hack at it.

Gradually, a hole emerged. The more she worked, the more her energy was restored. She worked harder. Unexpectedly, she broke through. A scent of beaver wafted up. It made her almost shout with joy. She had uncovered the vent hole. The mud had been plastered over—and poorly at that.

Working fast now, Poppy dug out the vent hole to its fullest. Done, she sat back, breathless with her efforts. Now there was nothing to prevent her from at least trying to get to Rye, force open his cage, and free him. Then she recalled that one of the reasons she had wanted Thistle and Curleydock to join her was to help with the bars. There was nothing to do but go on. She and Rye would have to get him free on their own.

Feeling almost reckless now, Poppy tied one end of the vine to a stick, took the free end in her mouth, and crept into the vent hole.

Even though she had made her way through the hole before, this time the way seemed longer. Moreover, some of the mud from the top had fallen in. She was constantly scraping it away and pushing it behind her.

Down she went. When she finally reached the end, she peered into the lodge. To her horror, the beavers were not sleeping. They were having a meeting.

Mr. Canad was standing before his family. Next to him was his daughter, Clara. With great glee, she was telling them what had happened out on the pond.

"I don't think any of them survived," she said with pride. "And it only took one smack of the old tail."

The other beavers beat their own tails against the ground. Even Mr. Canad joined in.

"Okay, folks, I just went out to check for myself. Clara did a great job, but if seeing is believing, the mice up on the hill are up to no good around that boulder. That's where we're going to put in a new dam.

"What Clara discovered suggests they've got something up their sleeves. Maybe they're trying to pull the wool over our eyes. Okay. I say it's time we pulled out all the stops. End our kid-glove treatment. Teach the whole kit and caboodle a trick or two. Knock the spots off them. Lower the boom.

"Let's go up there and give them a few what-fors. Level the playing field with our tails. Do I have any volunteers?"

There was an enthusiastic chorus of yea-sayers.

"Good!" Mr. Canad enthused. "Let's hit the water running. I'll lead you myself."

"Don't you think we should post some guards around by the waterway entry?" Clara asked. "Just in case they try something funny again."

"Good thinking, sweetheart. You're a chip off the old block. And for a beaver, you can't do better than that! We'll leave some guards here. Just in case."

High in the vent hole, Poppy heard it all. Although she was relieved the beavers were going, she worried about what was happening up by the nest.

She watched as the beavers scrambled out of the lodge.

Soon only two remained.

It had been Poppy's intention to crawl down the vine—just as she had done on her previous visit. Then, the beavers all had been asleep. This time, the two beavers who stayed in the lodge were not just awake, one of them went over to the cage where Rye was being kept.

"What are you doing?" called the other beaver.

"Just checking to make sure this guy's secure."

"Is he?"

"A sure thing."

The two beavers waddled away from the cage and lay down near the lodge's water entry to guard it.

Poppy watched them intently. Their backs were to her.

In the dimness—the fireflies were not very active—Poppy was sure she saw Rye. He was curled up in a tight ball at the far end of his cage. Even as she watched him, he got up and crept to one of the back bars. There he crouched. If she was seeing clearly, he was gnawing on one of them.

Just to see Rye working made Poppy's heart swell with love. Her doubts melted away. Together—somehow—they would get him out of the cage and to freedom. Her pulse quickened.

After giving a yank to the vine to make sure it would hold fast, Poppy began to lower it slowly. As she did, she kept her eyes on the two beavers. If they saw what she was doing, all was lost. She barely dared to breathe.

Inch by inch the vine dropped.

One of the beavers swung about and used a rear leg to scratch himself vigorously. Poppy froze. But the beaver's face was so scrunched up—he seemed to be enjoying his scratching—he gave no sign that he noticed anything unusual.

Poppy lowered the vine some more. She was pretty sure she had guessed its length properly, that it would touch the floor. She was wrong. Even when she had lowered the vine as far as possible, it hung off the ground by a distance—as best Poppy could reckon—twice her full height when she stood tall. At first dismayed, she decided it did not matter. It was—it had to be—close enough.

The next step would be harder. It was time for her to go down. Head first or tail first? She glanced over at the beavers. They were paying no attention. Best to go tail first. If the need came, heading up would be easier and faster than backing up.

After wiping her sweaty paws on her fur, Poppy grasped the vine and began her descent by letting herself drop in a series of small jerks.

The moment she left the vent hole in the ceiling, the vine began to sway. The farther she went, the greater the sway. It made her dizzy, then nauseated. She knew then she should have come down headfirst like the first time.

Squeezing her eyes shut, Poppy continued down. Moving with her eyes closed gave her a panicky feeling— far worse than the dizziness. She opened them in haste and hung there. The vine swayed. Her dizziness increased. Gritting her teeth, she made herself go on.

As she moved, she kept looking around at the beavers. They had remained quite still. It was just as she reached the halfway point that they showed signs of activity.

One of them got up and arched his back. Then he turned fully around. Poppy almost fainted with fright. But the beaver turned back around and resumed guarding the entryway. Never had Poppy felt so glad to be so small.

Poppy struggled to suppress her anxiety and move faster. A little calmer, she continued down.

She had reached the vine's end. Now she was dangling above the floor. There she hung, swaying back and forth, her heart beating madly. After taking one more look at the beavers, she released her grip and dropped to the floor.

The second she landed, she crouched down into as tight a ball as she could. Then, with great care, she lifted her head to check what the beavers were doing. They had not noticed her.

With a burst she sprang up and darted to the cage. "Rye," she called in a whisper even as she clung to the bars.

Rye looked up. "Poppy!" he gasped and fell back.

"*Shhh!*" she warned.

"You are always such a wonderful surprise," he said.

In spite of herself, Poppy grinned.

"Poppy . . . ?"

"Yes?"

"I've . . . I've been working on a poem about you. Would you like to hear it? It goes,

> "*Hail, sweet mouse of shape divine!*
> *Who pledged her heart and tail to me*
> *and mine . . .*"

"Rye," Poppy interrupted, "it sounds beautiful, but there's no time for that now. We need to get you out of here, fast."

"I'm all for that," Rye agreed. "I've been working away on this bar, too. It is awfully tough. Almost as hard as writing a good poem. And they do watch me. But I did make some progress. Poem and bar. Maybe the two of us can do the rest. The bar, that is."

"Show me where."

"Here." He went to the back of the cage. Poppy, on the outside, followed him. "This one."

Poppy looked at the twig. It was gnawed almost halfway through.

"Makes my teeth sore," Rye said.

"If you gripped from above," Poppy suggested, "and I held on from below, and we pulled in opposite directions, it might give."

"We can try."

The two mice did what Poppy suggested.

"Pull!" Rye urged. The two yanked. There was some give but not enough.

"Again," Rye said.

The twig splintered with a sudden snap. While it did not break completely in two, it had been pulled wide enough to allow Rye to squeeze through. He popped out and gave Poppy a hug. She returned it.

"Do you want to hear the rest of the poem?" he asked.

"Let's get out of here first."

"Of course. How silly of me. How did you come in?"

"The vent hole and another vine. A much longer one. Come on."

With Poppy in the lead, the two mice crept across the floor of the lodge.

As they went Poppy kept darting glances at the beavers.

Rye, following Poppy, kept thinking, "Isn't she amazing. Isn't she something."

They were halfway to the vine when one of the beavers turned, looked at them, saw what had happened, and cried, "Mice on the loose!"

CHAPTER 26

The Battle of the Boulder

WHAT HAD HAPPENED to Thistle and Curleydock?

When Thistle, under attack from the beaver, lost her grip on the raft, she let herself sink below the water's surface. A good swimmer, she had the sense to move fast and far away from the tumbled raft as well as the beaver. For as long as her lungs allowed her to, she swam underwater. Then she rose to the surface and cried out, "Curleydock! Poppy!"

There was no reply. And it was too dark to see anything.

Terribly distressed, Thistle swam about in circles, in search of her companions. She was still searching when she heard a faint splash.

"Who's that?" she called.

"It's me, Curleydock! Who's that?"

"Thistle."

"Where are you?"

"Here. Keep talking. Try to swim toward me. I'll try to move toward you."

The two met in the middle of the pond.

"Where's Poppy?" was the first thing Curleydock said.

"I hoped she'd be with you."

"I didn't see what happened to her."

"Do you think she's all right?" asked Thistle.

"I don't know."

"Listen!"

There came what sounded like a faint cry.

"Here we are!" Thistle called back loudly.

"*Shhh*! A beaver might hear you."

In any case, there was no response.

"Curleydock?"

"What?"

"Poppy said she wasn't that good a swimmer."

"Do . . . do you think . . ." Curleydock stammered, "do you think she . . . drowned?"

Instead of replying, Thistle said, "We'd better get back to the land."

"Which way?"

Thistle tried to gauge their place. "I think that way is closest." She pointed the way with her nose.

The two mice swam steadily. Neither spoke until they reached the shore. As soon as they got out they both looked back over the pond.

"Do you see anything?" Thistle said.

"No."

"What are we going to tell Pa and Ma?"

"Better just say what happened," Curleydock replied.

"What do you think . . . did happen?"

"She must have . . . drowned."

Thistle shook her head.

Curleydock said, "She said she couldn't swim. And we didn't hear her, did we?"

"Maybe she got to the lodge anyway."

"Thistle, even if she did, she said she needed us to get Rye out."

"But . . . then . . . what'll happen to Rye?"

There was no answer.

Suddenly Thistle said, "Curleydock, Ma and Pa were moving tonight. We don't know where they went."

"Maybe they left a note."

The two mice ran up the hill.

There was pale light—but no sun yet—upon the eastern horizon when an exhausted Thistle and Curleydock, full of their awful news, reached the hilltop. To their complete surprise, they saw the entire family working in a frenzy. Half were laboring in the ditch before the boulder. The others were toiling about the boulder's base, hauling away dirt as fast as they could. Most of the earth around the boulder already had been removed. To Thistle and Curleydock's eyes the boulder appeared to be resting on absolutely nothing.

"Pa!" Curleydock called.

Valerian turned. His mouth opened with surprise. "Why . . . what are you two doing here? Did you free Rye? Where's Poppy?"

"Pa," Thistle said, "we were getting close to the beaver's lodge—on a raft—when one of the beavers discovered us."

"No!"

"Then we got whacked with a tail," Curleydock continued. "The raft went over. But we're . . . Thistle and I . . .
we're good swimmers."

"You mean . . . Poppy . . . ?"

"We're not sure, but . . . drowned, probably."

Valerian, mouth agape, struggled to control his emotions.
Turning away, he gazed at the boulder, the ditch, the pond.

"Pa," Thistle asked, "what's everybody doing?"

Valerian explained as best he could.

"You're going to smash the dam?" Curleydock exclaimed
when he heard the plan.

"We're trying. But I think I'd better talk to your mother.
Tell her your news." He hurried away.

Clover, to oversee her part of the digging, had estab-
lished herself—with her three youngest—just behind the
large stone.

The moment Valerian appeared, she bolted up. "What is
it? Something has happened. I can see it in your face."

"It's Thistle and Curleydock—"

Clover shut her eyes.

"They were going to the lodge on a wood chip when a
beaver turned them over."

"Valerian . . . the children . . . what happened to them?"

"Thistle and Curleydock got back. They're good swimmers.
But it's Poppy. They don't know what happened to her."

"Then they never reached . . . Rye?"

"No."

"Valerian!"

"Clover," Valerian asked, "what do you think we should do?"

Clover dipped her head, swallowed hard, then looked up. "Valerian, you said it before: Poppy's a clever mouse. Maybe she's all right. Maybe she isn't. But I still think we have to get that boulder going down the ditch like we planned. We have to do . . . *something*."

"But Clover, if Rye's still in the lodge . . . it might make things worse."

The two mice stared at each other.

"Valerian," Clover said in a whisper, struggling to remain dry eyed, "I still think we have to try. *I do*."

"I guess you're right," Valerian returned grimly. "The ditch is pretty much done. How soon can we push the boulder down?"

Clover, burping one of the babies, said, "We only need to dig a little more and then—"

Whatever Clover was about to say was cut off by a shout on the other side of the hill. "Beavers!" came the cry. "The beavers are attacking!"

"Oh, my gosh! Work as fast as you can!" Valerian urged Clover. "We'll try to hold them off." He gave Clover a quick hug, then tore around to the front of the boulder to see what was happening.

Thirteen beavers had waddled out of the pond. Arrayed all in a row, dripping wet, they were whacking their broad tails on the earth, making an awful racket. Their teeth, side by side, looked like an orange picket fence.

In the middle of the line was Mr. Canad, peering up at the boulder. Now that the mice's work had progressed so far, he was able to grasp what it was the mice were attempting.

"Great balls of fire!" he raged. "They're going to topple that boulder. If it comes down, it'll hit the dam. It's unfair! It's wrongheaded! It's a matter of life or death!"

Up he reared. "For the honor of Canad's Cute Condos," he bawled, "we've got to draw the line somewhere. Give me a dam or give me death! Go whole hog! Go for broke! Fight tooth and tail! Charge!" As one, the beavers began to waddle up the hill.

The mice, taken by surprise, stopped work on the boulder and the ditch. Too terrified to do anything, they simply stared at the advancing line of beavers.

Valerian rushed down. "Defend yourselves!" he cried. "If only for a few minutes. That's what we need."

Galvanized, the mice scrambled in all directions, running and tripping over themselves as they gathered up sticks, pebbles, and clods of dirt.

"Hold your fire," Valerian cried. "Wait till you can see the gap between their teeth."

The beavers, beating their tails, pressed up the hill. Their sheer bulk was enough to frighten away some of the mice.

Curleydock, unable to restrain himself, charged down the hill with a mud ball in either paw. "Come on," he called. "Don't stand there. Attack!"

Thistle, armed with a pointed stick, was the first to join him.

As soon as he was in throwing range, Curleydock chucked his mud balls at the beavers. When these balls bounced harmlessly off the beavers' pelts, he gathered up more and threw them.

Unfazed, the beavers continued their advance. "Be warned!" Mr. Canad bawled up at the mice. "We don't intend to let anything happen to that boulder!"

Valerian, meanwhile, was in a frenzy, organizing his sons, daughters, and grandchildren into three brigades.

"When I give the word," he told them, "the first group will follow me. Go after one beaver at a time. It's the only way. You other two groups, attack when you think it's time. Now, chins up, whiskers straight, noses aquiver! Let's show them what mice can do!"

Brandishing a twig, he dashed down the hill, his off-

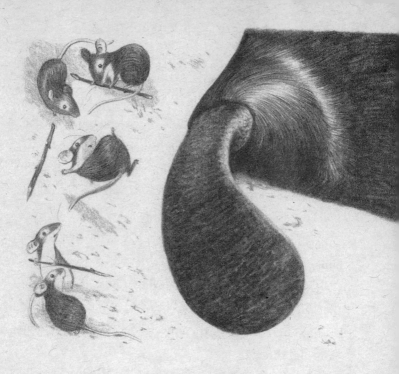

spring trailing close behind.

Thistle and Curleydock were off on their own, poking and pricking a beaver's feet with twigs. Maddened, the beaver spun about, lowering his tail shield. Brother and sister pressed their attack relentlessly. The beaver turned and fled back to the pond.

Meanwhile, Valerian and his pack of mice surrounded another beaver. They pelted her with mud balls, then followed up with a stick attack. The beaver responded by

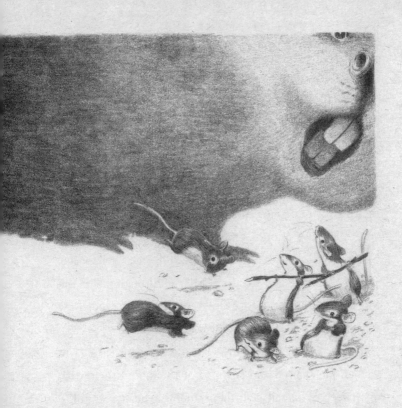

grabbing at them, snatching them up and flinging them off to one side. She also began to flail about with her tail, smashing down indiscriminately.

The mice, some hurt, retreated.

But even as they did, the second wave of mice—fifteen strong and squeaking madly—swarmed down the hill. "Mice to the fore! Mice to the fore!" they cried in unison. So furious was their onslaught—with sticks, pebbles, and mud balls—the attack of the beavers faltered. When one of the mice managed to shove a stick up a beaver's nose, the beaver turned and scampered back toward the pond.

Mr. Canad reared up to block his way. "How dare you retreat," he cried, shoving the frightened beaver back up the hill. "They're only mice. Beavers never retreat! We have not yet begun to fight! Rally round the flag! Don't give up the ship. Remember Canad's Cute Condos. You're fighting for the honor and glory of me!"

A third wave of mice, emboldened by the success of the first two groups, poured down the hill in a great wave, squealing, "Mice and freedom! Mice and freedom!" at the top of their lungs. Too excited to stay organized, they struck out at any beaver that was near.

It was Thistle and Curleydock who went after Mr. Canad. He snarled and snapped at them, and then, with one sweep of his tail, sent them tumbling head over tail.

Dazed but unhurt, they shook themselves up, then hurled themselves back into the fray. WHACK! WHACK! went Mr. Canad's tail. The mice danced away.

The mice did manage to dent the beavers' onslaught. Each beaver—surrounded by mice—was forced into fighting alone. But though the mice attacked and attacked again, the beavers gradually moved up the hill. Despite their stubborn resistance, the mice were forced into retreat. It was not a rout, but their strength was beginning to ebb.

Valerian, who was engaged with a particularly large beaver, had been knocked down twice. Each time he picked himself up, he cast an eye toward the top of the hill. When he saw that Clover and the other mice were still feverishly digging around the boulder, he threw himself back into the fray.

Clover, who kept looking from the frantic digging around the boulder to the equally frantic battle below, finally shouted, "We're ready!" down to Valerian.

Valerian, who had just been brushed back, staggered up, heard the call. "Mice to the boulder!" he bellowed. "Mice to the boulder!"

The mice began an orderly retreat. But the beavers, sensing success, pressed harder, gnashing their orange teeth and smacking their tails down indiscriminately. "Drive them away!" Mr. Canad shouted. "Show no mercy! Flatten them! Turn them into lily pads!"

The attack worked. The mice began to scatter. Once dispersed, they grew panicky. They started to race in all directions. Now their orderly retreat became a rout.

"Swat them!" Mr. Canard cried. "Crush them! Flatten them out!"

Valerian raced toward the boulder. A blow from Mr. Canad sent him backward. Spinning about in corkscrew fashion, he collapsed to his knees, stunned.

Mr. Canad reared up and beat his chest. "We have

them!" he cried triumphantly. "Strike while the iron is hot. Hit them where it hurts. Winning isn't everything, it's the only thing!"

Suddenly, from up behind the boulder came a great shout: "What the mice mollies is going on here? Where's Poppy? Get out of my way, fur face! Hit the road, tooth brain."

There was the sound of a slap, and a beaver—his nose a pincushion of quills—let forth a shriek, and began to bolt down the hill.

"Who's in charge here?" Ereth yelled. "Where's that seed brain, Poppy? Get out of my way, waffle tail!" WHACK! Another beaver went scrambling down the hill. "Beat it, buck tooth!"

Thistle approached him. "You are good. Just like Poppy said."

"Don't call me good, you furry inch of tail leavings. Just tell me what's going on. What's all this ruckus? Who are you, chisel mouth?" he demanded.

"The name is Caster P. Canad. But please, just call me Cas. We can be friends. You know what the philosopher

said, A stranger is just someone you haven't met. I mean that, sin—"

"Don't tell me I'm your friend, buster!" Ereth interrupted with a roar. "I'm nobody's friend!" With that he slapped Mr. Canad hard, right across the face, with his quill-covered tail. For a moment, Mr. Canad, nose bristling with quills, could do no more than stare at Ereth with shock, horror, and pain. Then he turned and fled down the hill toward the pond. Seeing their leader in a humiliating retreat, the rest of the beavers quickly lost heart and followed.

"Tumble the boulder!" Valerian cried. "Hurry!"

Regrouping, the mice raced up to the top of the hill. Some forty of them, including Clover, dug their rear toes into the earth and placed their front paws against the boulder.

"Push!" Clover cried.

The boulder trembled.

"Push!" she cried again.

The boulder shook. It moved. It began to roll forward. Quickly it gathered speed and momentum until, to the high, shrill cheers of the mice, the boulder plopped into Valerian's ditch. Then, still rolling, it began to hurtle down the hill, moving faster and faster. Plummeting, it struck a stone, which caused the boulder to bounce high into the air, over the heads of the astonished and retreating beavers. When it came down, it struck the dam.

There was a tremendous THUMP! followed by absolute silence. The silence was broken by a sudden gurgling noise—the sound of the pond water emptying through the breach in the dam.

Neither beavers nor mice spoke. They could only stare.

It was Ereth who broke the profound silence by asking, "Where the busted bat bung is that Poppy, anyway?"

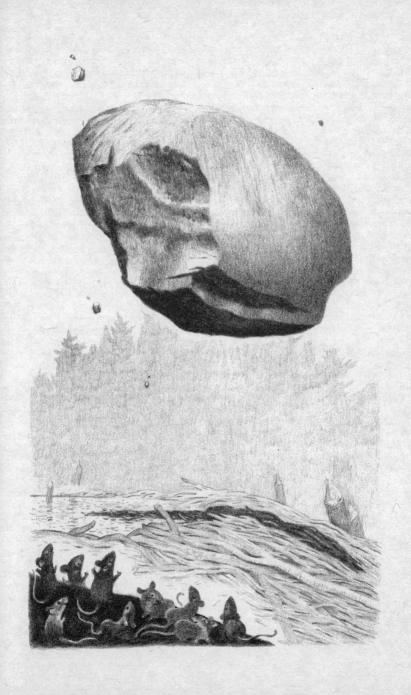

CHAPTER 27

Inside the Lodge
(continued)

WHEN THE FIRST BEAVER cried out a warning that Rye was escaping, the second one spun about.

"Run!" Poppy cried and headed straight for the vine. Rye tore after her.

Poppy reached the vine first. She made a flying leap, grabbed it, swung wildly, steadied, then began to haul herself paw over paw until she made herself stop and see where Rye was.

To her horror she saw that Rye had not reached the vine. Moreover, one of the beavers had gotten to the center of the lodge first and was blocking his way. The other beaver, meanwhile, was circling behind him.

"There's one behind you!" Poppy called.

Rye spun about, saw the beaver, and darted toward the side of the lodge.

Meanwhile the beaver just below the vine stood up and tried to grab Poppy.

Scrambling higher, she managed to elude the beaver's claws. The beaver responded by grabbing hold of the vine and yanking, pulling it all down, including Poppy.

Down Poppy plummeted, landing with a thump on the soft floor of the lodge where she lay, dazed.

The vine, as it fell, dropped around the beaver. When the beaver tried to get rid of it, he became thoroughly entangled.

Rye, watching Poppy fall, gasped. Though the other beaver was coming right at him, he made a U-turn and shot back toward her. The beaver pursuing him was thrown off. She swiped at him but missed.

Rye approached the first beaver. Realizing that he was still enmeshed in the vine, Rye ran forward and reached Poppy's side.

Poppy struggled woozily to get up.

Rye helped her. "Come on!" he cried, and led her back toward the broken cage.

The beaver entangled in the vine tore free. He hurried to where the other beaver was. Together they went after the mice, certain they had them cornered. Moving carefully, not wishing to miss their chance, they slowed down and began to creep forward.

"Are you all right?" Rye asked Poppy. He was whispering.

"I think so."

"What should we do?"

Poppy twisted around. The beavers were approaching. "I'll act as if I'm hurt," she said, her voice low but urgent.

"Why?"

"Let them get close to us, then we'll race off."

"Which direction?"

"Doesn't matter."

"Poppy, they'll trap us. It would be better if we split, you right, me left. We'll meet at the water entry. We can swim from there."

"Rye," Poppy cried, "I *can't* swim. I was lucky the first time."

"Don't worry. I'll be with you."

"Rye . . ."

"There's no other way out," Rye insisted. "I'll be with you. The vine is down."

"But . . ."

"Here they come!"

The two mice approached the back wall. There they turned and waited. Poppy, keeping a wary eye, rubbed a leg as if it hurt. Rye acted as if he were tending to his friend.

The beavers advanced, sweeping wide to prevent any escape.

"Is your head clear?" Rye whispered Poppy. "Can you do it?"

"I think so. But Rye, swimming . . ."

"*Shhh!* Here they come."

As the beavers advanced, Rye and Poppy pressed their backs against the wall.

"Don't try to escape!" one of the beavers called. "Just slip into the cage. Both of you. If you do, we won't hurt you." They lumbered forward.

Just as they were about to grab the mice, Rye shouted, "Go!" The two mice tore off in opposite directions.

The beavers, taken by surprise, lunged forward, but missed.

Rye and Poppy, racing in separate paths, reached the far

sides of the wall. They cut across to the shelf that hung out over the waterway.

Rye was ready to dive in. Poppy held back. Rye looked behind. The beavers, furious at being tricked again but seeing where the mice were perched, galloped across the center of the lodge in pursuit.

"Jump in!" Rye called.

"I can't," Poppy cried. "I'll drown. I know I will."

"You must."

Poppy braced herself, ready to do what she knew she had to do.

Suddenly, from outside the lodge there was a great THUMP. The entire lodge shook.

Both mice and beavers stopped and looked around.

"What was that?" Rye asked, awed.

"I'm not sure," Poppy replied, equally startled.

The next moment there was a great gurgling sound. Poppy and Rye looked down into the water entry. To their astonishment the water was draining swiftly away. Nothing was left but mud.

"The water's gone!" Poppy called.

She jumped off the shelf and landed in the mud and sprinted down the tunnel.

Rye followed.

When the beavers reached the shelf, they looked with

amazement at the empty waterway. "Come on! You heard what Cas said, 'Hit the water running.'"

"But it's mud!"

"They'll get away."

The beavers leapt. Bigger and heavier than the mice, they sank deep into the mud. "Help! Help!" they cried. But the more they struggled, the more they sank. They dared not move, but could only wait and watch the mice scamper off to freedom.

CHAPTER 28

Farewells

WITH THE DAM BROKEN, the Brook soon resumed its calm, meandering state. The water cleared, the water-logged banks dried. Almost overnight new, green shoots sprang up. Lilies quickly reestablished themselves. Once again butterflies and dragonflies danced lazily over the languid mirror surface.

The beavers retreated far up the Brook. No one saw anything more of them—not their teeth, their tails, or their dams—or heard their thoughts.

Within a week, Poppy and Rye were married by the mice's old nest, which, after it had dried out, had been reclaimed by Valerian and Clover.

It was Valerian and Clover who, according to mouse custom, performed the marriage ceremony. Thistle and Curleydock held a canopy of wildflowers over their heads—another mouse tradition. The rest of the mouse family were in full attendance, giggling and laughing, squeaking and chatting, endlessly talking among themselves. As part of the ceremony Rye read all thirty-two stanzas of his poem in praise of Poppy.

She was charmed.

Before the wedding took place, Poppy went to ask Ereth to be "best porcupine." The old fellow—who had retreated to a clump of trees beyond the ridge—refused with surly indignation.

"I'd rather wait here," he grumbled.

"It would mean so much to me if you were there," Poppy pressed.

"It would mean more to me if you *weren't* there," Ereth retorted.

Poppy considered him carefully. "Ereth, you never told me what you wanted to say back in the thicket."

"Forget it," he muttered.

"Ereth," she said, "I know you don't want me to say it, but you really are the greatest and sweetest of porcupines. And the ultimate best friend to have come back."

"I only came because I couldn't find my way home to Dimwood Forest," Ereth sneered. "I needed to get you to get me back home."

"But you did do good," Poppy insisted. "If you hadn't come, the beavers would have won."

"Beavers . . ." Ereth grumbled. "Bunch of furry-faced chisels."

"Well," Poppy said, "I still wish you'd come to the wedding." And before Ereth knew what she was doing, she went up to him and kissed him on the nose.

"Mouse mush . . ." Ereth muttered. As Poppy went away he started to rub the kiss away, but suddenly changed his mind. Instead, he sat for a long while, cross-eyed, staring at his nose.

Once the marriage ceremony was over, Rye announced that he and his bride would be leaving the woodlands and going to Dimwood Forest to Poppy's home. The couple invited the family to visit as often as possible, and promised to return when they could.

Poppy made her own good-bye. "I have loved two of your sons," she told Valerian and Clover. "What fine parents you are. We can only hope to do the same."

They all hugged one another—with such a large family it took a long time—and then, side-by-side, Rye and Poppy hurried up the hill.

Ereth was waiting.

"Did you get stuck together?" he asked sourly.

"It was a beautiful ceremony," Poppy said. "I would have loved you to have been there."

"*Love,*" Ereth sneered. "The less said about all that slop, the better. Come on. Let's go home."

They started off. Early on, however, they came to the meadow where Poppy and Rye had first met, and danced.

Rye looked at Poppy. Poppy looked at Rye. They did not need to say a word. They held up their paws and began to dance upon the meadow. They dipped, they jumped, they swayed, they twirled and whirled.

Ereth, keeping his distance, watched from afar. Though he tried to hide it, the old porcupine allowed himself a small, hidden smile—and a tear. Catching himself, he frowned and turned his back on the dancers. "*Love*," he complained bitterly. "Nothing but slug splat stew and toad jam. Phooey!"

But—Ereth never did wash his nose.

What begins as Ereth the prickly old porcupine's loneliest birthday ever becomes his greatest adventure in ERETH'S BIRTHDAY, the fourth book of the Poppy stories!

FROM *Ereth's Birthday*

— CHAPTER I —

A Special Day

IN DIMWOOD FOREST, in the dark, smelly log where the old porcupine Erethizon Dorsatum lived, Ereth—as he preferred to call himself—woke slowly.

Not the sweetest smelling of creatures, Ereth had a flat face with a blunt, black nose and fierce, grizzled whiskers. As he stirred, he rattled his sharp if untidy quills, flexed his claws, yawned, frowned, and grumbled, "Musty moose marmalade," only to suddenly remember what day it was and smile. Today was his birthday.

Ereth had given very little thought to what *he* would do about the day. As far as he was concerned, his birthday meant others would be doing something for *him*. And the one he was quite certain would be doing all the providing was his best friend, Poppy.

Poppy, a deer mouse, lived barely an acorn toss from Ereth's log in a gray, lifeless tree—a snag with a hole on one side. She resided there with her husband, Rye, and their eleven children.

Ereth, in a *very* private sort of way, loved Poppy. Enough for him to live near her. He had never told anyone about this love, not even her. But since the porcupine was certain that Poppy thought of him as her best friend, he assumed she would be making a great fuss over his birthday. A party, certainly. Lavish gifts, of course. Best of all, he would be the center of attention.

So it was that when Ereth waddled out of his log that morning he was surprised not to find Poppy waiting for him. All he saw were her eleven children playing about the base of the snag, squeaking and squealing uproariously.

"Why can't young folks ever be still?" A deeply disappointed Ereth complained to himself. "Potted pockets of grizzly grunions, it would save so much trouble if children were born . . . old."

Agitated, he approached the young mice. "Where's your mother?" he barked. "Where's your wilted wet flower of a father?"

"They . . . went . . . looking for . . . something," one of them said.

Though Ereth's heart sank, he made a show of indifference by lifting his nose scornfully and moving away from the young mice.

Snowberry, one of the youngsters, glanced anxiously around at the others, then cried out, "Good morning, Uncle Ereth!"

This greeting was followed by the ten other young mice singing out in a ragged, squeaky chorus, "Good morning, Uncle Ereth!"

Ereth turned and glowered at the youngsters. "What the tiddlywink toes do you want?" he snapped.

"Aren't you going to stay and play with us, Uncle Ereth?" Snowberry called.

"No!"

"Why?"

"I'm . . . busy."

"You don't look busy."

"I'm trying to find some peace and quiet," Ereth snapped. "With all the noise you make, buzzard breath, what else do you think I'd be doing?"

One of the mice—her name was Columbine—slapped a paw over her mouth in order to keep from laughing out loud.

Ereth glared at her. "What are you laughing at?"

"You," Columbine sputtered. "You always say such funny things!"

"Listen here, you smidgen of slipper slobber," Ereth

fumed. "Don't tell *me* I talk funny. Why don't you stuff your tiny tail into your puny gullet and gag yourself before I flip you into some skunk-cabbage sauce and turn you into a pother of butterfly plunk?"

Instead of frightening the young mice, Ereth's outburst caused them to howl with glee. Sassafras laughed so hard he fell down and had to hold his stomach. "Uncle Ereth," he cried, "you are so hilarious! Please say something else!"

"Belching beavers!" Ereth screamed. "I am not hilarious! You're just a snarl of runty seed suckers with no respect for anyone older than you. How about a little consideration? As far as I'm concerned you mice have as much smarts as you could find in a baby bee's belly button."

"But you *are* funny, Uncle Ereth," cried another of the young mice, whose name was Walnut. "Nobody else talks like you do. We love it when you swear and get angry at us."

"I am not angry!" Ereth raged. "If I were angry, I'd turn you all into pink pickled pasta so fast it would make lightning look like a slow slug crawling up a slick hill. So listen up, you tub of tinsel twist."

This was too much for the young mice. They laughed and squeaked till their sides ached.

"Uncle Ereth," said Sassafras between giggles, "please— *please*—say something funny again. You are the funniest animal in the whole forest!"

Staring wrathfully at the young mice, Ereth considered uttering something unbelievably disgusting—dangling doggerels—thought better of it, and wheeled about, heading north as fast as he could.

"Uncle Ereth!" the mice shouted after him. "Please stay and say something else funny. *Please* don't go!"

But Ereth refused to stop.

Sassafras watched the porcupine plunge into the forest, then turned to the others. "But what are we going to tell Mom and Dad?" he cried. "They told us to make sure he didn't go anywhere."

"Oh, don't worry," Columbine assured her brother. "Uncle Ereth always comes back."

CHAPTER 2

Ereth Makes a Decision

"Kids," Ereth muttered as he hurried away. "They think they're so wonderful. Truth is, they do nothing but make their elders work hard, eat their food, ask for things, break them, then proclaim all adults stupid! And what do kids give in return? Nothing!

"All that baby-sitting I do . . . all that listening to their endlessly boring stories, dumb jokes, what they learned today . . . hearing Poppy and Rye talk about this one's problems, that one's doings . . . attending their parties . . . finding presents for them . . .

"Well, here it is, *my* birthday. At least I only have one a year. But do those kids notice? No! Not so much as a gill of grasshopper gas. Do they care what I feel, think, am? Not one pinch of pith pills! Right! The whole world would be better off without kids. So all I say is, keep kids to the rear, blow wind, and turn on the fan!"

With such thoughts and words churning in his mind, Ereth rushed on. Once, twice, he passed a rabbit, a squirrel, a vole, but when they saw the mood the porcupine was in they retreated quickly, not willing even to call a greeting. After all, the creatures of Dimwood Forest knew Erethizon Dorsatum quite well. Very few had any desire to interfere with him when he was in one of his bad moods— which was clearly the case that morning.

The old porcupine pressed on, his mind taken up by a careful composition of the things he hated, the insults he had endured, the slights he had suffered. The list was very long. The more he recalled, the grumpier he became, and the faster he hurried on.

It was an hour before Ereth allowed himself to pause. All his emotion and running had quite worn him out and made him ravenous. Spying a young pine tree, he scrambled over to it and began to peel away the outer bark, then chew on the green layer underneath.

"Good, good," he babbled as he gobbled. "This is more like it."

Suddenly he lifted his nose, sniffed, and frowned. "Squirrel-splat soup! The air has changed."

It was true—the air *was* different. It had become crisp and had a deep, tangy smell. And now that Ereth thought about it, the days had been growing shorter, the nights longer. It was only a question of when the first snow would arrive.

"Seasons," Ereth thought to himself. "Boiled bat butter! Just when you get used to one way, everything changes. Why can't things ever stay the way they are? Phooey and fried sala-mander spit with a side order of rat ribbon. I hate change!"

More than ever, Ereth was convinced that he needed *something* to mark the day. But what? It had to be something special. Something just for him. Then, in a flash, he knew exactly what would please him most. *Salt.*

Just to think about salt turned Ereth's longing into deep desire and dreamy drools. For Ereth, salt was the most delicious food in the whole world. He could shut his eyes and almost taste it. Oh, if only he had a chunk! A piece! Even a *lick* of salt would salvage the day. No, there was nothing he would not do for the smallest bit of it.

The old porcupine sighed. Since no one else was going to pay attention to him, he owed it to himself to find *some* birthday treat, and salt was the perfect thing. But where was he going to find any?

Though Ereth, with his great knowledge of Dimwood Forest, knew exactly where *he* was, finding salt was quite another mat-ter. He considered New Farm, a place where some humans kept a whole block of salt in the middle of a lawn. Once, when the block had shattered and fallen to the ground, Ereth had gorged himself for days. Though truly fabulous, that salt was long gone.

Moreover, when the humans replaced the block they put it at a height convenient for deer—not porcupines.

"Deer dainties!" Ereth snarled with contempt. "Why couldn't they have put the salt out for *me*?"

So the question remained, Where could Ereth find salt?

Then Ereth remembered: on the far northern side of Dimwood Forest was a lake. Long Lake, the animals called it. On its shore humans had built a log cabin. Rather crudely constructed, it did not even sit on the earth, but on a platform a few feet off the ground. The cabin was used rarely, only when humans wanted to hunt or trap animals. Every year brought frightening stories of deer, fox, and rabbits, among others, being killed, hurt, or maimed by these humans. Hardly a wonder that the cabin—though more often than not deserted— was a place the animals of Dimwood Forest avoided. Just thinking about it made Ereth shudder. And yet . . .

As Ereth also knew, these humans often left traces of salt on the things they used. Sometimes it was nothing more than a smear of sweat on the handle of a tool, a canoe paddle, or an odd bit of clothing like a hatband. These objects were often stored in that space beneath the cabin.

Scanty though these tastings were, they were tempting enough for Ereth to venture to the log cabin now and again to satisfy his salt cravings. Once he had been rewarded by finding an almost full bag of salty potato chips. That was a day to remember.

Hardly a wonder then, that just the possibility of finding even a lick of salt stirred Ereth.

He looked around. Overhead loomed the great trees that kept the ground dim and gave the forest its name. Such sky as he could see was gray, while the sun itself seemed to have turned dull. White mist curled up from the earth's murky nooks and crannies.

"It's almost winter," Ereth told himself. "This may be my last chance to get salt for a while. Besides," he reminded himself yet again, "it's my birthday. I deserve something special."

Even so, the porcupine hesitated, all too aware of the risks involved. Fooling around with humans, especially if they were hunters or trappers, was risky.

"Bug bubble gum," he swore. "What do I care if there are humans at the cabin? Nothing scares *me*."

With that thought Ereth continued making his way in a northerly direction toward Long Lake, the cabin, and the salt.

ALSO BY AVI